PENGUIN CLASSICS
The Two-Penny Bar

T0249260

'I love reading Simenon. He makes me think of Chekhov'
— William Faulkner

'A truly wonderful writer . . . marvellously readable – lucid, simple, absolutely in tune with the world he creates'
— Muriel Spark

'Few writers have ever conveyed with such a sure touch, the bleakness of human life'
— A. N. Wilson

'One of the greatest writers of the twentieth century . . . Simenon was unequalled at making us look inside, though the ability was masked by his brilliance at absorbing us obsessively in his stories'
— *Guardian*

'A novelist who entered his fictional world as if he were part of it'
— Peter Ackroyd

'The greatest of all, the most genuine novelist we have had in literature'
— André Gide

'Superb . . . The most addictive of writers . . . A unique teller of tales'
— *Observer*

'The mysteries of the human personality are revealed in all their disconcerting complexity'
— Anita Brookner

'A writer who, more than any other crime novelist, combined a high literary reputation with popular appeal'
— P. D. James

'A supreme writer . . . Unforgettable vividness'
— *Independent*

'Compelling, remorseless, brilliant'
— John Gray

'Extraordinary masterpieces of the twentieth century'
— John Banville

ABOUT THE AUTHOR

Georges Simenon was born on 12 February 1903 in Liège, Belgium, and died in 1989 in Lausanne, Switzerland, where he had lived for the latter part of his life. Between 1931 and 1972 he published seventy-five novels and twenty-eight short stories featuring Inspector Maigret.

Simenon always resisted identifying himself with his famous literary character, but acknowledged that they shared an important characteristic:

> My motto, to the extent that I have one, has been noted often enough, and I've always conformed to it. It's the one I've given to old Maigret, who resembles me in certain points . . . 'understand and judge not'.

Penguin is publishing the entire series of Maigret novels.

GEORGES SIMENON

The Two-Penny Bar

Translated by DAVID WATSON

Previously published as The Bar on the Seine

PENGUIN BOOKS

PENGUIN CLASSICS

Published by the Penguin Group

Penguin Books Ltd, 80 Strand, London WC2R ORL, England

Penguin Group (USA) Inc., 375 Hudson Street, New York, New York 10014, USA

Penguin Group (Canada), 90 Eglinton Avenue East, Suite 700, Toronto, Ontario, Canada M4P 2Y3
(a division of Pearson Penguin Canada Inc.)

Penguin Ireland, 25 St Stephen's Green, Dublin 2, Ireland (a division of Penguin Books Ltd)

Penguin Group (Australia), 707 Collins Street, Melbourne, Victoria 3008, Australia
(a division of Pearson Australia Group Pty Ltd)

Penguin Books India Pvt Ltd, 11 Community Centre, Panchsheel Park, New Delhi – 110 017, India

Penguin Group (NZ), 67 Apollo Drive, Rosedale, Auckland 0632, New Zealand
(a division of Pearson New Zealand Ltd)

Penguin Books (South Africa) (Pty) Ltd, Block D, Rosebank Office Park, 181 Jan Smuts Avenue,
Parktown North, Gauteng 2193, South Africa

Penguin Books Ltd, Registered Offices: 80 Strand, London WC2R ORL, England

www.penguin.com

First published in French as *La Guinguette à deux sous* by Fayard 1932
This translation first published as *The Bar on the Seine* in Penguin Books 2003, and revised 2014

012

Copyright 1932 by Georges Simenon Limited
Translation copyright © Georges Simenon Limited, 2003, 2014
GEORGES SIMENON ® Simenon.tm
MAIGRET ® Georges Simenon Limited
All rights reserved

The moral rights of the author and translator have been asserted

Set in 12.5/15pt Dante MT Std
Typeset by Palimpsest Book Production Ltd, Falkirk, Stirlingshire
Printed and bound in Great Britain by Clays Ltd, Elcograf S.p.A.

ISBN: 978-0-141-39417-6

www.greenpenguin.co.uk

Contents

1. *Saturday with Monsieur Basso*

A radiant late afternoon. The sunshine almost as thick as syrup in the quiet streets of the Left Bank. And everything – the people's faces, the countless familiar sounds of the street – exuded a joy to be alive.

There are days like this, when ordinary life seems heightened, when the people walking down the street, the trams and cars all seem to exist in a fairy tale.

It was 27 June. When Maigret arrived at the gate of the Santé prison he found the guard gazing soppily at a little white cat that was playing with the dog from the dairy.

Some days the pavement must be more resonant underfoot: Maigret's footsteps echoed in the vast courtyard. He walked to the end of a corridor, where he asked a warder:

'Does he know? . . .'

'Not yet.'

A key turned in the lock. The bolt was pulled back. A high-ceilinged cell, very clean. A man stood up, looking unsure as to which expression to adopt.

'All right, Lenoir?' the inspector asked.

The man nearly smiled. But a thought came into his mind and his face hardened. He frowned suspiciously, and his mouth twisted into a sneer for a moment or two. Then he shrugged his shoulders and held out his hand.

'I see,' he said.

'What do you see?'

A resigned smile.

'Give it a rest, eh? You must be here because . . .'

'I'm here because I'm off on holiday tomorrow and . . .'

The prisoner gave a hollow laugh. He was a tall young man. His dark hair was brushed back. He had regular features, fine brown eyes. His thin dark moustache set off the whiteness of his teeth, which were as sharp as a rodent's.

'That's very kind of you, inspector . . .'

He stretched, yawned, put down the lid of the toilet in the corner of the cell which had been left up.

'Excuse the mess . . .'

Then suddenly, looking Maigret in the eye, he said:

'They've turned down the appeal, haven't they?'

There was no point in lying. He knew already. He started pacing up and down.

'I knew they would . . . so when is it? . . . Tomorrow?'

Even so, his voice faltered and his eyes drank in the glimmer of light from the narrow window high up the cell wall.

At that moment, the evening papers being sold on the café terraces announced:

The President of the Republic has rejected the appeal of Jean Lenoir, the young leader of the Belleville gang. The execution will take place tomorrow at dawn.

It was Maigret himself who had arrested Lenoir three months previously, in a hotel in Rue Saint-Antoine. A split second later and the bullet the gangster fired at him would have caught him full in the chest rather than ending up lodged in the ceiling.

In spite of this, the inspector bore him no grudge; indeed, he had taken something of a shine to him. Firstly, perhaps, because Lenoir was so young – a twenty-two-year-old who had been in and out of prison since the age of fifteen. But also because he had a self-confidence about him.

He had had accomplices. Two of them were arrested at the same time as him. They were both guilty and on this occasion – an armed robbery – they probably played a bigger part than the boss himself. However, Lenoir got them off the hook. He took the whole blame on himself and refused to 'spill the beans'.

He never put on an act, wasn't too full of himself. He didn't blame society for his actions.

'Looks like I've lost,' was all he said.

It was all over. More precisely, it would be all over when the sun, which was casting a golden strip of light on the cell wall, next rose.

Almost unconsciously, Lenoir felt the back of his neck. He shivered, turned pale, gave a derisive laugh:

'It feels weird . . .'

Then suddenly, in an outburst of bitterness:

'There are others who deserve this, and I wish they were going down with me!'

He looked at Maigret, hesitated, walked round the narrow cell once more, muttering:

'Don't get excited, I'm not going to put anyone in the frame now . . . but all the same . . .'

The inspector avoided looking at him. He could feel a confession coming. And he knew the man was so prickly that the slightest reaction or sign of interest on his part would make him clam up.

'There's a little place known as the "Two-Penny Bar" . . . I don't suppose you're familiar with it, but if you happen to find yourself in the neighbourhood you might be interested to know that one of the regulars there has more reason than me to be putting his head on the block tomorrow . . .'

He was still pacing up and down. He couldn't stay still. It was hypnotic. It was the only sign of his inner turmoil.

'But you won't get him . . . Look, without giving anything away, I can tell you this much . . . I don't know why this is coming back to me now. Maybe because I was just a kid. I couldn't have been more than sixteen . . . Me and my friend used to do a bit of filching around the dance halls. He must be in a sanatorium by now – he already had a cough back then . . .'

Was all this talk just to give himself the illusion of being alive, to prove to himself that he was still a man?

'One night – it must have been around three in the morning – we were walking down the street. It doesn't matter which street. Just a street. We saw a door opening ahead of us. There was a car parked by the roadside. This guy came out, pushing another guy in front of him. No, not pushing. Imagine you're carrying a shop dummy and trying to make it look like it's your friend walking next to you. He put him in the car and got into the driver's seat. My friend shot me a look and we both jumped up on to the rear bumper. In those days they called me the Cat . . . that tells you all you need to know! The guy drove all over the place. He seemed to be looking for something, but seemed to keep losing his way. In the end we realized what he'd been looking for, because we arrived at the Canal Saint-Martin. You've worked it out, haven't you? It was over in the time it takes to open and shut a car door. One body at the bottom of the canal . . .

'Smooth as you like! The guy in the car must have put lead weights in the stiff's pockets, because he sank like a stone.

'We kept our cool. Another wink and we're back on the bumper. Then it was just a case of checking the client's address. He stopped in the Place de la République to have a glass of rum at the only café that was open. Then he drove his car to the garage and went home. We could see his silhouette through the curtains as he got undressed . . .

'We blackmailed him for two years, Victor and me. We were novices. We were afraid of asking for too much . . . a few hundred at a time . . .

'Then one day he moved house, and we lost him . . . Then three months ago I ran into him again at the Two-Penny Bar. He didn't even recognize me . . .'

Lenoir spat on the ground, automatically searched his pockets for his cigarettes.

'You'd think they'd let me smoke, in my situation,' he muttered.

The shaft of sunlight above their heads had disappeared. Footsteps could be heard out in the corridor.

'It's not that I'm making out that I'm better than I am, but this guy I'm telling you about should be up there with me, tomorrow, on the . . .'

Suddenly the beads of sweat stood out on his forehead, and his legs buckled. He sat down on the edge of his bunk.

'Leave me . . .' he sighed. 'No, don't . . . don't leave me alone today . . . It's better to talk to someone . . . Hey, do you want me to tell you about Marcelle, the woman who . . .'

The door opened. The prisoner's lawyer hesitated when he saw Maigret. He had pasted on his professional smile, so that his client wouldn't be able to guess that his appeal had been turned down.

'I have good news . . .' he began.

'I know!'

Then, to Maigret:

'Guess I won't be seeing you, inspector . . . Well, we've all got a job to do. By the way, I wouldn't bother checking out the Two-Penny Bar. This guy is just as cunning as you . . .'

Maigret offered his hand. He saw his nostrils twitch, his dark moustache moisten with sweat, the two front teeth biting the lower lip.

'Better this than typhoid!' Lenoir joked, with a forced laugh.

Maigret didn't go away on holiday; there was a case involving forged bonds that took up nearly all of his time.

He had never heard of the Two-Penny Bar. He asked around among his colleagues.

'Don't know it. Whereabouts? On the Marne? The lower Seine?'

Lenoir was sixteen at the time of the events he had described. So the case was six years old, and one evening Maigret read the reports for that year.

There was nothing sensational. Missing persons, as always. A woman chopped up into pieces, whose head was never found. As for the Canal Saint-Martin, it had thrown up no less than seven corpses.

The forged bonds turned out to be a complicated case, involving many lines of inquiry. Then he had to drive Madame Maigret to her sister's in Alsace, where she stayed for a month every year.

Paris was emptying. The asphalt grew sticky underfoot. Pedestrians sought the shady side of the street, and the café terraces were full.

Expecting you Sunday without fail. Love from everyone.

Madame Maigret's summons arrived when her husband had failed to turn up for a fortnight. It was Saturday, 23 July. He tidied up his desk and warned Jean, the office boy at the Quai des Orfèvres, that he probably wouldn't be back before Monday evening.

As he was about to leave, he noticed the brim of his bowler, which had been torn for weeks. His wife had told him a dozen times to buy a new one.

'You'll have people throwing you coins in the street . . .'

He spotted a hatshop in Boulevard Saint-Michel. He tried on a few, but they were all too small for his head.

'I'm sure this one will be just right . . .' the spotty young shop assistant kept insisting.

Maigret was never more miserable than when he was trying things on in shops. In the mirror he was looking in, he spotted a man's back and head, and on the head a top hat. As the man was dressed in hunting tweeds, he cut a rather droll figure.

'No! I wanted something a bit older-looking,' he was saying. 'It's not meant to be smart.'

Maigret was waiting for the assistant to return from the back of the shop with some new hats for him to try on.

'It's just for a little play-acting . . . a mock marriage which we're putting on with a few friends at the Two-Penny Bar . . . there'll be a bride, mother of the bride, page-boys, the lot! . . . Just like a village wedding! . . . Now do you see what I'm after? . . . I'm playing the part of the village mayor . . .'

The customer gave a hearty laugh. He was about thirty-five, thickset, with rosy cheeks; he had the air of a prosperous businessman.

'Maybe one with a flat brim . . .'

'Hold on! I think we've got just the thing you're after in the workshop. It was a cancelled order . . .'

Maigret was brought another pile of bowlers. The first one he tried on fitted. But he dallied and made sure he left the shop just before the man with the opera hat. He hailed a taxi, just in case he needed it.

He did. The man came out of the shop, got into a car

parked next to the pavement and drove off in the direction of Rue Vieille-du-Temple.

There he spent half an hour in a second-hand shop and emerged with a flat cardboard box, which obviously contained a suit to go with his top hat.

Then on to the Champs-Élysées, Avenue de Wagram. A small bar on a street corner. He stayed there only five minutes and left accompanied by a buxom, jovial-looking woman who must have been in her thirties.

Twice Maigret looked at his watch. His first train had already gone. The second would be leaving in a quarter of an hour. He shrugged his shoulders and told the taxi driver:

'Keep following him.'

Much as he had expected, the car drew up in front of an apartment block on Avenue Niel. The couple hurried in through the entrance. Maigret waited a quarter of an hour, then went in, taking note of the brass plate:

Bachelor apartments by the month or by the day.

In a smart office which had a whiff of adultery he found a perfumed manageress.

'Police! . . . The couple who just came in here . . .'

'Which couple?'

But she didn't put up much of a struggle.

'Very respectable people, both married. They come twice a week . . .'

On his way out, the inspector glanced through the car windscreen at the identity plate.

Marcel Basso,
32, Quai d'Austerlitz, Paris.

Not a breath of wind. The air was warm and heavy. All the trams and buses heading for the railway stations were packed. Taxis full of deckchairs, fishing-rods, shrimp nets and suitcases. The asphalt glistened blue, and the café terraces resounded with the clatter of saucers and glasses.

'After all, three weeks ago Lenoir was . . .'

There hadn't been much talk about it. It was an everyday case – he was what you might call a professional criminal. Maigret remembered the quivering moustache and sighed as he looked at his watch.

Too late now. Madame Maigret would be waiting with her sister at the barrier of the little station that evening and would not fail to mutter:

'Always the same!'

The taxi driver was reading a newspaper. The man with the top hat left first, scanned the street both ways before signalling to his companion, who was lurking in the entrance.

They stopped in Place des Ternes. He saw them kiss through the rear windscreen. They were still holding hands after the woman had hailed a taxi and the man was ready to drive off.

'Do you want me to follow?' the driver asked Maigret.

'Might as well.'

At least he'd found someone who knew the Two-Penny Bar!

Quai d'Austerlitz. A huge sign:

Marcel Basso
Coal importer – various sources
Wholesale and retail
Domestic deliveries by the sack
Special summer prices

A yard surrounded by a black fence. On the opposite side of the street a quayside bearing the firm's name, with moored barges and a newly unloaded pile of coal.

In the middle of the yard a large house, in the style of a villa. Monsieur Basso parked his car, automatically brushed his shoulders to remove any female hairs and went into his house.

Maigret saw him reappear at the wide-open window of a room on the first floor. He was with a tall, attractive blonde woman. They were both laughing and talking in an excited fashion. Monsieur Basso was trying on his top hat and looking at himself in the mirror.

They were packing suitcases. There was a maid in a white apron in the room.

A quarter of an hour later – it was now five o'clock – the family came downstairs. A boy of about ten led the way, brandishing an air rifle. Then came the servant, Madame Basso, her husband, a gardener carrying the cases . . .

The group was brimming with good humour. Cars drove past, heading for the country. At Gare de Lyon the specially extended holiday trains whistled shrilly.

Madame Basso got in next to her husband. The boy climbed into the back seat among the cases and lowered the windows. The car was nothing fancy, just a standard family car, dark blue, nearly new.

A few minutes later they were driving towards Villeneuve-Saint-Georges. Then they took the road towards Corbeil. They drove through the town and ended up on a potholed road along the bank of the Seine.

Mon Loisir

That was the name of the villa, on the river between Morsang and Seine-Port. It looked newly built, bricks still shiny, the paintwork fresh, flowers in the garden that looked as if they had been washed that morning. A diving-board over the river, rowing-boats by the bank.

'Do you know the area?' Maigret asked his driver.

'A bit . . .'

'Is there somewhere to stay around here?'

'In Morsang, the Vieux-Garçon . . . Or further on, at Seine-Port, Chez Marius . . .'

'And the Two-Penny Bar?'

The driver shrugged.

The taxi was too conspicuous to stay there much longer by the roadside. The Bassos had unloaded their car. No more than ten minutes had elapsed before Madame Basso appeared in the garden dressed in a sailor's outfit, with an American naval cap on her head.

Her husband must have been more eager to try out his fancy dress, for he appeared at a window buttoned up in an improbable-looking frock coat, with the top hat perched on his head.

'What do you reckon?'

'Shouldn't you be wearing the sash?'

'What sash?'

'Mayors all wear a tricolour sash . . .'

Canoes glided slowly by on the river. In the distance, a tug blew its siren. The sun was sinking behind the trees on the hillside further downstream.

'Let's try the Vieux-Garçon!' said Maigret.

The inn had a large terrace next to the Seine. Boats of all sorts were moored to the bank, while a dozen or so cars were parked behind the building.

'Do you want me to wait for you?'

'I don't know yet.'

The first person he met was a woman dressed all in white, who almost ran into him. She was wearing orange blossom in her hair. She was being chased by a young man in a swimming-costume. They were both laughing. Some other people were observing the scene from the front steps of the inn.

'Hey, keep your dirty paws off the bride!' someone shouted.

'At least until after the wedding!'

The bride stopped, out of breath, and Maigret recognized the lady from Avenue Niel, the one who visited the apartment with Monsieur Basso twice a week.

A man in a green rowing-boat was putting away his fishing tackle, his brow furrowed, as if he were performing some delicate and difficult operation.

'Five Pernods, five!'

A young man came out of the inn, his face plastered

with greasepaint and rouge. He was made up to look like a freckly, ruddy-cheeked peasant.

'What do you think?'

'You should have red hair!'

A car arrived. Some people got out, already dressed up for the village wedding. There was a woman in a puce silk dress which trailed along the ground. Her husband had stuffed a cushion under his waistcoat to simulate a paunch and was wearing a boat chain that was meant to look like a watch chain.

The sun's rays turned red. The leaves on the trees barely stirred. A canoe drifted downstream; its passenger, stripped to the waist, sat at the back, doing no more than lazily steer it with a paddle.

'What time are the carriages due to arrive?'

Maigret hung around, feeling out of place.

'Have the Bassos arrived?'

'They passed us on the way!'

Suddenly, someone came and stood in front of Maigret, a man of about thirty, already nearly bald, his face made up like a clown's. He had a mischievous glint in his eyes. He spoke with a pronounced English accent:

'Here's someone to play the notary!'

He wasn't completely drunk. He wasn't completely sober, either. The rays of the setting sun turned his face purple; his eyes were bluer than the river.

'You'll be the notary, won't you?' he asked with the familiarity of a drunkard. 'Of course you will, old chap. We'll have a great time.'

He took Maigret's arm and added:

'Let's have a Pernod.'

Everyone laughed. A woman muttered:

'He's got a nerve, that James.'

But James wasn't bothered. He dragged Maigret back to the Vieux-Garçon.

'Two large Pernods!'

He was laughing at his own little joke as they were served two glasses full to the brim.

2. The Lady's Husband

By the time they got to the Two-Penny Bar, things hadn't yet clicked for Maigret, as he liked to say. He hadn't had any high hopes in following Monsieur Basso. At the Vieux-Garçon he had looked on gloomily as the people milled about. But he hadn't felt that nibble, that little shift, the 'click' that told him he was on to something.

While James was forcing him to have a drink with him, he had seen customers come and go, helping each other to try on their ridiculous costumes, laughing, shouting. The Bassos had turned up, and their son, whom they had made up as a carrot-headed village idiot, had gone down a storm.

'Don't mind them,' said James each time Maigret turned round to look at the group. 'They're having a good time and they're not even drunk . . .'

Two carriages had drawn up. More shouting. More laughing and jostling. Maigret sat next to James, while the landlord, his wife and the staff of the Vieux-Garçon lined up on the terrace to see them off.

The sun had given way to a blue-tinted twilight. The lights from the windows of the quiet villas on the far bank of the Seine glimmered in the dusk.

The carriages trundled onwards. The inspector took in the scene around him: the coachman, whom everyone teased and who responded with a laugh through gritted teeth; a young girl who had made herself up as the simple country lass, and who was trying to put on a peasant accent; a grey-haired man dressed like a granny . . .

It was all very confusing. Such an unexpected mix of people that Maigret could scarcely work out who went with whom. He needed to get things in focus.

'See her over there? That's my wife . . .' James told him, pointing out the plumpest of the women, who was wearing leg-of-mutton sleeves. He said this in a cheerless tone, with a glint in his eyes.

They sang. They passed through Seine-Port, and people came out on to their doorsteps to watch the procession go by. Little boys ran after the carriages for some distance, whooping with delight.

The horses slowed to walking pace. They crossed a bridge. A sign could just about be made out in the half-light:

Eugène Rougier – Licensee

A tiny little whitewashed house squeezed in between the towpath and the hillside. The lettering on the sign was crude. As they approached, they could hear snatches of music, interspersed with a grinding noise.

What was it that finally clicked? Maigret couldn't put his finger on it. Perhaps the mildness of the evening, the little white house with its two lighted windows and the contrast with this invading circus troupe?

Perhaps the couple who came forward to see the 'wedding party' – the man a young factory worker, the woman in a pink silk dress, standing with her hands on her hips . . . ?

The house had only two rooms. In the one on the right, an old woman was busy at her stove. In the one on the left could be seen a bed, some family portraits.

The bistro was at the back. It was a large lean-to with one wall completely open to the garden. Tables and benches, a bar, a mechanical piano and some Chinese lanterns. Some bargees were drinking at the bar. A girl of about twelve was keeping an eye on the piano, occasionally rewinding it and slipping two sous into the slot.

The evening got going very quickly. No sooner had the new arrivals climbed down from the carriages than they cleared away the tables and started dancing, calling for drinks. Maigret had lost sight of James and found him again at the bar, lost in thought over a Pernod. The waiters were laying the tables outside under the trees.

One of the carriage drivers moaned: 'I hope they don't keep us too late! It's Saturday! . . .'

Maigret was alone. Slowly, he turned full circle. He saw the little house with its plume of smoke, the carriages, the lean-to, the two young lovers, the crowd in fancy dress.

'This is it,' he murmured to himself.

The Two-Penny Bar! The name might refer to the poverty of the establishment, or perhaps to the two coins you had to put into the mechanical piano to make it work.

And somewhere here there was a murderer! Perhaps one of the wedding party! Perhaps the young factory hand! Perhaps one of the bargees!

Where was James? Where was Monsieur Basso? . . .

There was no electric lighting. The lean-to was lit by two oil lamps, and other lamps on the tables and in the garden, so the whole scene was a patchwork of light and dark.

'Come on . . . food's ready!'

But they carried on dancing. A few people must have been knocking back the aperitifs, for within a quarter of an hour there was a distinctly drunken atmosphere in the place.

The old woman from the bistro waited at the tables herself, anxious that the food was going down well – salami, then an omelette, then rabbit – but no one cared much. They hardly noticed what they were eating. And everyone wanted their glass refilled.

A noisy hubbub, drowning out the music. The bargees at the bar watched the goings-on and carried on their meandering conversation about the canals of the North and electric haulage systems.

The two lovers danced cheek to cheek, but they couldn't take their eyes away from the tables where all the merrymaking was going on.

Maigret didn't know anyone. He was sitting next to a woman who had a ridiculous painted moustache and beauty spots dabbed all over her face, who for some reason kept calling him Uncle Arthur.

'Would you pass the salt, Uncle Arthur? . . .'

Everyone was on first-name terms. There was much backslapping and ribbing going on. Was this a group of people who knew each other well? Or just a crowd that had been thrown together by chance?

And what did they do in real life? For example, the grey-haired man dressed as the granny?

Or the woman dressed up as a little girl, who spoke in a falsetto voice?

Were they middle-class like the Bassos? Marcel Basso was sitting next to the bride. They weren't flirting. Occasionally they exchanged a meaningful glance that probably meant:

'This afternoon was good, wasn't it?'

Avenue Niel, in a furnished apartment! Was her husband here too?

Someone let off a firecracker. A Bengal light was lit in the garden, and the young couple watched it tenderly, hand in hand.

'It's just like in a theatre,' said the pretty girl in pink.

And there was a murderer!

'Speech! . . . Speech! . . . Speech!'

Monsieur Basso got to his feet, a beaming smile on his face. He coughed, pretended to be embarrassed and began an absurd speech that was interrupted by rounds of applause.

Now and again his eye fell on Maigret. His was the only serious face around the tables. And Maigret sensed the man's discomfort as he turned his head away. Nevertheless, his gaze returned to Maigret twice, three times more, questioning, troubled.

'. . . and I'm sure you'll join me in a toast: to the bride!'

'To the bride!'

Everyone stood up. People kissed the bride, clinked

glasses. Maigret saw Monsieur Basso go over to James and ask him a question. No doubt it was:

'Who's that?'

He heard the reply:

'I don't know . . . just a pal . . . He's fine . . .'

The tables had been abandoned. Everyone was dancing in the lean-to. A small group of people, barely distinguishable from the tree trunks in the dark, had gathered to watch the fun.

Corks were popping.

'Come and have a brandy!' said James. 'I guess you aren't a dancer.'

What an odd fellow! He had already drunk enough to lay out four or five normal men, but he wasn't really drunk. He just slouched around, looking sour, not joining in. He took Maigret back into the house. He sat in the landlord's high-backed armchair.

A stooping old woman was doing the washing-up while the landlord's wife, who didn't look far off fifty, and who was no doubt her daughter, busied herself around the kitchen.

'Eugène! . . . Another six bottles of bubbly . . . It might be a good idea to ask the coachman to go and fetch some more from Corbeil.'

A country cottage interior, very poor. A pendulum clock in a carved walnut case. James stretched out his legs, picked up the bottle of brandy he had ordered and poured out two glasses.

'Cheers . . .'

The sound of the voices and the music were now a

distant hubbub. Through the open door they could see the fast-moving current of the Seine.

'Little cubby holes for canoodling couples,' said James contemptuously.

He was thirty years old. But it was obvious he wasn't the canoodling type.

'I bet they're at it already at the bottom of the garden . . .'

He watched the old woman bent double over her washing-up.

'Here, give me a tea towel.'

He started drying the glasses and dishes, pausing only to take a swig of cognac.

Now and again someone passed by the door. Maigret took advantage of a moment when James was talking to the old woman to slip away. He'd only gone a few paces out of the door when someone asked him for a light. It was the grey-haired man in the woman's dress.

'Thanks . . . You don't dance either?'

'Never!'

'Not like my wife, then. She hasn't missed a single dance.'

'The bride?'

'Yes . . . And when she does stop, she'll catch her death . . .'

He gave a sigh. He looked grotesque, a serious-looking middle-aged man in an old woman's dress. The inspector wondered what he did in real life, what he normally looked like.

'I feel like we've already met,' he said casually.

'Me too . . . I've seen you somewhere before . . . But where? . . . Maybe you've bought a shirt in my shop . . .'

'You're a haberdasher?'

'On the Grands Boulevards . . .'

His wife was now making more noise than anyone. She was obviously drunk, and was becoming quite over-exuberant. She was dancing with Basso and was clinging to him so tightly that Maigret turned away in embarrassment.

'A funny little girl,' the man sighed.

Little girl! This thirty-year-old, buxom woman with her sensual lips and her come-hither look, now throwing her-self at her gentleman partner.

'She's a bit wild once she gets going . . .'

The inspector looked at his companion, unable to tell whether he was being angry or affectionate.

At that moment someone shouted:

'They're off to the bridal chamber! . . . Take your places, everyone! . . . Where's the bridegroom? . . .'

The bridal chamber was a small outhouse at the end of the lean-to. Someone got the door open, someone else went to find the bridegroom at the end of the garden.

Maigret was observing the real husband, who was smil-ing.

'First the garter!' someone shouted.

It was Monsieur Basso who removed the garter, cut it up into small pieces and distributed them among the crowd. The bride and groom were bundled into the out-house and the door locked behind them.

'She's enjoying herself . . .' murmured Maigret's com-panion. 'Are you married yourself?'

'Oh, yes . . .'

'Is your wife here?'

'No . . . she's on holiday.'

'Does she like being with young people too?'

Maigret couldn't tell if he was being serious or teasing. He took advantage of a lapse in conversation to cross the garden, passing close to the factory worker and his girl-friend, who were pressed up against a tree.

In the kitchen James was talking pleasantly with the old woman while drying glasses, and emptying them.

'What's going on?' he asked Maigret. 'Have you seen my wife?'

'I haven't noticed her.'

'Hard to miss her, surely.'

The night wound down quickly. It must have been around one in the morning. Some people started talking about making a move. Someone was being sick by the river. The bride had regained her freedom. Only the younger members of the group were still dancing.

The carriage driver came up to James.

'Do you think it'll be much longer? The old woman's been waiting for me for an hour . . .'

'You're married too?'

So James rounded everyone up. In the carriages, some people started nodding off to sleep, while others were trying to keep the party spirit going, singing and laughing with varying degrees of conviction.

They passed a line of sleeping barges. A train whistled in the distance. They slowed down when they reached the bridge.

The Bassos got out at their villa. The haberdasher had already left the group at Seine-Port. A woman was whispering to her husband, who was drunk:

'I'll tell you tomorrow what you got up to! . . . Shut up! . . . I'm not listening! . . .'

The sky was sprinkled with stars, which were reflected in the water of the river. At the Vieux-Garçon, everyone was asleep. Handshakes all round.

'Are you coming sailing tomorrow?'

'We're going fishing.'

'Goodnight.'

A row of bedrooms. Maigret asked James:

'Is one of these for me?'

'Take your pick! . . . See if you can find an empty one . . . If not, you can always sleep in my room.'

Lights went on in a few windows. The sound of shoes being dropped on the floor. The squeak of bedsprings. A couple whispered loudly in one of the rooms. Perhaps the woman who had a thing or two to say to her husband?

It was eleven o'clock in the morning. Now they all looked like themselves. It was hot and sunny. The waitresses dressed in black and white bustled round the terrace, laying tables.

The group began to reassemble. Some were still in pyjamas, others in sailors' outfits, others still in flannels.

'Hung over?'

'Not too bad . . . And you?'

Some had already set off to go fishing, or had already

returned. There were some small sailing-dinghies and canoes.

The haberdasher was wearing a well-tailored grey suit. Clearly a man who liked to appear well-groomed in public. He spotted Maigret and came over.

'Allow me to introduce myself: Monsieur Feinstein . . . I mentioned my shop yesterday . . . My professional name is Marcel.'

'Did you sleep well?'

'No, I didn't! As I thought, my wife had made herself ill . . . It's always the same . . . She knows she doesn't have a robust constitution . . .'

Why did he seem so interested in Maigret's reaction?

'Have you seen her this morning?'

He looked around and finally spotted her in a sailing-boat with four or five people in bathing costumes. Monsieur Basso was at the helm.

'Is this your first visit to Morsang? . . . It's very nice. You'll want to come back, you'll see . . . We'll have the place to ourselves . . . Just the usual crowd, friends . . . Do you play bridge?'

'Oh . . . a bit . . .'

'We'll be having a game later . . . Do you know Monsieur Basso? . . . One of the biggest coal merchants in Paris . . . A splendid chap! . . . That's his dinghy coming in now . . . Madame Basso is very sporty.'

'And James?'

'Already on the booze, I shouldn't wonder. It's all he lives for. And he's still a young man, he could be doing something with his life. He'd rather take it easy. He works for an English bank in Place Vendôme. He's been offered loads of jobs, turned them all down. He insists on finishing work at four so he can hit the bars in Rue Royale.'

'And that young man over there – the tall one?'

'The son of a jeweller.'

'And the man over there fishing?'

'Runs a plumbing business. He's the keenest fisherman in Morsang. Some of us play bridge, others like fishing, others prefer sailing. It all makes for a good crowd. Some people have their own villas out here.'

In the distance, at the first bend in the river, stood the tiny white house. One could just make out the lean-to with its mechanical piano.

'Does everyone go to the Two-Penny Bar?'

'It's been our haunt for the last two years. James was the one who discovered it. Before that it was just used by workers from Corbeil, who came here to dance on Sundays. James used to slip off there for a quiet drink when things got too boisterous around here. One day the gang went with him, had a bit of a dance, and that's how it all started. We've pretty much taken over the place . . . the former clientele has more or less drifted away.'

A waitress walked by with a tray full of aperitifs. Someone dived into the river. A frying smell came from the kitchen.

And there was smoke rising from the chimney of the Two-Penny Bar. A face came to Maigret's mind: thin, dark moustache, pointed teeth, quivering nostrils . . . Jean Lenoir pacing up and down to hide his fear, talking about the Two-Penny Bar.

'There are others who deserve this, and I wish they were going down with me!'

But the next day, at the crack of dawn, he was alone. No one from the bar was there with him.

Despite the heat, Maigret felt a sudden chill. And he looked at this dapper haberdasher with his gold-tipped cigarette with fresh eyes. Then he turned to where the Bassos' boat was being moored at the bank, half-naked people leaping ashore to greet their friends with handshakes.

'May I introduce you to our friends?' said Monsieur Feinstein. 'Monsieur . . . ?'

'Maigret. I'm a civil servant.'

The introductions were very proper: short bows, exchanges of 'Pleased to meet you' and 'The pleasure is all mine'.

'You were there yesterday evening, weren't you? I thought the whole thing went splendidly. Are you playing bridge with us this afternoon?'

A thin young man came up to Monsieur Feinstein, took him to one side and spoke to him in a low voice. None of this was lost on Maigret. He saw Feinstein frown; he looked somewhat alarmed. He inspected Maigret from head to foot before adopting his normal demeanour.

The group went up to the terrace to find a table.

'Pernods all round? Hey, where's James?'

Monsieur Feinstein was edgy, despite his efforts to remain calm. He paid particular attention to Maigret.

'What are you drinking?'

'I don't mind.'

'You . . .'

His sentence tailed off, and he pretended that something else had caught his attention. After a pause, he tried coming from a different angle:

'It's odd that you should have landed up at Morsang . . .'

'Yes, very strange . . .' the inspector agreed.

The drinks were served. Everyone was talking over each other. Madame Feinstein had placed her foot on Monsieur Basso's, and her bright eyes were fixed on his.

'Such a lovely day. What a shame that the water is too clear for fishing.'

The air was clammy and still. Maigret remembered a shaft of sunlight penetrating a high white cell.

Lenoir walking and walking to forget that he wouldn't be walking for much longer.

And Maigret's gaze rested heavily on each face in turn: Monsieur Basso, the haberdasher, the businessman, James, who had just arrived, the young men and women . . .

He tried to picture each of them in turn, by the Canal Saint-Martin at night, carrying a corpse 'like a shop dummy and trying to make it look like it's your friend walking next to you'.

'Your good health,' said Monsieur Feinstein, maintaining his fixed smile for as long as he could.

3. The Two Boats

Maigret had lunch on his own on the terrace of the Vieux-Garçon. The rest of the group sat at adjoining tables, and the conversation flowed between them.

He had now established the social background of this crowd: tradesmen, owners of small businesses, an engineer, two doctors. They were people who owned their own cars, but who only had Sundays off for unwinding in the countryside.

They all owned boats – either motor-boats or small dinghies. They were all keen on fishing.

They lived here for twenty-four hours every week, dressed in their sailing gear, wandering around barefoot or in sandals. Some of them affected the rolling gait of old sea-dogs.

More couples than young people. They displayed the rather deep familiarity of people who have been spending every Sunday together for years.

James was everyone's favourite, the person who bound them all together. With his casual manner, his ruddy complexion and his dreamy eyes, he only had to make an appearance to put everyone in a good mood.

'How's the hangover, James?'

'I never get hangovers. If I feel queasy, I find a couple of Pernods usually sort it out.'

They started reliving the night before. They had a laugh about someone who had been sick, and another who had almost fallen into the Seine on the way back. Maigret was part of the group without really belonging. The previous evening, everyone had talked to him like an old friend; now they eyed him a little more cautiously, occasionally involving him in the conversation out of politeness.

'Do you like fishing?'

The Bassos were having lunch at home. The Feinsteins too, and a few others who had their own villas. Thus the group fell into two classes: those who owned villas and those who stayed at the inn.

Around two o'clock the haberdasher came to fetch Maigret; he seemed to have taken him under his wing.

'We're waiting for you to come and play bridge.'

'At your place?'

'At the Bassos'! We were supposed to play at my place today, but the maid is sick, so we'll be better off at the Bassos' . . . Are you coming, James?'

'I'll come in the boat.'

The Bassos' villa was a kilometre upstream. Maigret and Feinstein went on foot, while the rest went by dinghy or canoe.

'Basso's a fine fellow, don't you think?'

Maigret couldn't tell if he was being serious or not. He was a strange one. Neither one thing nor the other: neither old nor young, neither good-looking nor ugly; maybe without a single original thought in his head, yet maybe full of secrets.

'I expect we'll be seeing you every Sunday from now on?'

They came across groups of people picnicking, as well as fishermen every hundred metres or so along the river bank. It was getting hotter. The air was extraordinarily still and oppressive.

In the Bassos' garden wasps buzzed around the flowers. There were three cars parked there already. The young boy was playing by the riverbank.

'You're joining our game?' the coal merchant asked Maigret as he greeted him cordially. 'Excellent! In which case we don't need to wait for James. He'll never get any wind in his sail on a day like today.'

Everything was brand new. The villa was like a city dweller's fantasy: a profusion of red-checked curtains, old Norman furniture and rustic pottery.

The card table was set up in a living room that opened on to the garden through a large bay window. Bottles of Vouvray were chilling in an ice bucket frosted with condensation. Bottles of liqueur were set out on a tray. Madame Basso, dressed in a nautical outfit, did the honours.

'Brandy, *quetsche, mirabelle*? Unless you'd rather have a Vouvray?'

There were vague introductions to the other players, not all of whom had been present the night before, but who were still part of the Sunday crowd.

'Monsieur . . . er . . .'

'Maigret.'

'Monsieur Maigret, who plays bridge . . .'

It was almost like the set of a light opera, so vivid and spruce was the décor. Nothing to remind you of the serious business of life. The child had clambered into a white-painted canoe, and his mother called out:

'Be careful, Pierrot!'

'I'm going to meet James!'

'A cigar, Monsieur Maigret? If you prefer a pipe, there is some tobacco in this pot. Don't worry, my wife is used to it.'

Directly opposite on the other bank stood the Two-Penny Bar.

The first part of the afternoon passed uneventfully. Maigret noticed, however, that Monsieur Basso wasn't playing and that he appeared a little more on edge than this morning.

He didn't look like the nervous type. He was tall and well built and seemed to ooze vitality through every pore. A man who loved life, a rough and ready sort from sturdy working-class stock.

Monsieur Feinstein played bridge like a real aficionado and called Maigret to task on more than one occasion.

At around three o'clock the Morsang crowd began to fill the garden, and then the room where they were playing. Someone put on a record. Madame Basso poured out the Vouvray, and fifteen minutes later there were half a dozen couples dancing around the bridge players.

At that moment Monsieur Feinstein, who had seemed completely absorbed by the game, murmured:

'Hey, what's happened to our friend Basso?'

'I think I saw him get into a boat!' someone said.

Maigret followed the haberdasher's gaze to the opposite

bank of the river, where a small boat had just arrived right next to the Two-Penny Bar. Monsieur Basso climbed out of it and walked up towards the inn. He returned a short while later, looking preoccupied, despite his ostensible air of good humour.

Another incident which passed almost unnoticed. Monsieur Feinstein was winning at cards. Madame Feinstein was dancing with Basso, who had just come back. James, a glass of Vouvray in his hand, joked:

'Some people couldn't lose if they tried.'

The haberdasher didn't flinch. He dealt out the cards. Maigret was watching his hands, and they were as steady as ever.

Another hour or two went past. The dancers were getting tired. Some of the guests had gone for a swim. James, who had lost at cards, stood up and muttered:

'How about a change of scene? Anyone for the Two-Penny Bar?'

He bumped into Maigret on the way out.

'Come with me.'

He had reached that level of drunkenness that he never went beyond, no matter how much he drank. The others all stood up. A young man cupped his hands around his mouth and called out:

'Everyone to the Two-Penny Bar!'

'Careful you don't fall!'

James helped the inspector to climb into his six-metre sailing boat, pushed off with a boat-hook and sat down in the stern.

There wasn't a breath of wind. The sail flapped. They

struggled against the current, even though it was virtually non-existent.

'We're not in any hurry!'

Maigret saw Marcel Basso and Feinstein get into the same motor-boat, cross the river in no time and step out in front of the bar.

Then came the dinghies and the canoes. Though it had set out first, James's boat soon brought up the rear, because of the lack of wind, and the Englishman seemed reluctant to use the oars.

'They're a good bunch,' James suddenly murmured, as if following his own line of thought.

'Who?'

'All of them. They have such boring lives. But what can you do about that? Everyone's life is boring.'

It was ironic, for as he lolled in the back of the boat with the sun glinting off his bald pate, he looked supremely content.

'Is it true you're a policeman?'

'Who told you that?'

'I can't remember. I heard someone mention it. Hey, it's just a job like any other.'

James tightened the sail, which had caught a breath of wind. It was six o'clock. The Morsang clock was striking, and was answered by the one at Seine-Port. The bank was obstructed by reeds, which were teeming with insects. The sun was beginning to turn red.

'What do you . . .'

James's question was cut short by a sharp crack. Maigret leapt to his feet, almost overturning the boat.

'Look out!' his companion shouted. He threw his weight over to the other side, then grabbed an oar and started rowing. His brow was furrowed, his eyes wide with anxiety.

'It's not the hunting season yet.'

'It came from behind the bar!' said Maigret.

As they drew closer they could hear the tinkle of the mechanical piano and an anguished voice shouting:

'Turn the music off! Turn the music off!'

There were people running. A couple was still dancing, even after the piano was switched off. The old grandmother was coming out of the house, carrying a bucket in her hand. She stood stock-still, trying to work out what was going on.

Because of the reeds it was difficult to land. In his haste, Maigret stepped into the water up to his knee. James came after him with his supple stride, mumbling to himself inaudibly.

They only had to follow the group of people heading behind the lean-to that served as the dance hall. Round the back of the shed they found a man staring wide-eyed at the crowd, stammering over and over:

'It wasn't me! . . .'

It was Basso. He seemed unaware that he was holding a small, pearl-handled revolver in his hand.

'Where's my wife? . . .' he asked the people around him, as if he didn't recognize them.

Some people went to look for her. Someone said:

'She stayed at home to prepare dinner . . .'

Maigret had to push his way to the front before he saw

a figure lying in the long grass, dressed in a grey suit and a straw hat.

Far from being tragic, the scene had an air of absurdity, with everyone standing around not knowing what to do. They stood there looking in bewildered fashion at Basso, who seemed just as bewildered as they.

To cap it all, one of the members of the group, who was a doctor, was standing right next to the body but hadn't made a move. He was looking at the others, as if waiting for instructions.

There was, however, a small moment of tragedy after all. The body suddenly twitched. The legs seemed to be trying to bend. The shoulders twisted back. A part of Monsieur Feinstein's face came into view. Then, as if in one last effort, he stiffened, then slowly became immobile.

The man had just died.

'Check his heart,' Maigret told the doctor curtly.

The inspector, who was not unfamiliar with such events, caught every detail of the scene. He saw everything at once, with an almost unreal clarity.

Someone had fallen to the ground at the back of the crowd, wailing piteously. It was Madame Feinstein, who had been the last to arrive because she had been the last to stop dancing. Some people were bending over her. The landlord of the bar was approaching with the suspicious expression of a distrustful peasant.

Monsieur Basso was breathing quickly, pumping air into his lungs. He suddenly noticed the revolver in his clenched fist. He appeared stupefied. He looked at each of the persons around him in turn, as if wondering to whom he should give the gun. He repeated:

'It wasn't me . . .'

He was still looking round for his wife, despite what he had been told.

'Dead,' said the doctor as he stood up.

'A bullet?'

'Here . . .'

And he pointed to the wound in the side, then looked round for his own wife, who was dressed in only a swimming-costume.

'Do you have a telephone?' Maigret asked the landlord.

'No. You have to go to the station . . . or up to the lock.'

Marcel Basso was wearing white flannel trousers, and his shirt was partly unbuttoned, showing off the broadness of his chest.

He rocked slightly on his feet, reached out a hand as if looking for some support, then suddenly slumped down in the grass less than three metres from the corpse and laid his head in his hands.

The comic note returned. A thin female voice piped up:

'He's crying! . . .'

She thought she was whispering, but everyone heard.

'Do you have a bicycle?' Maigret asked the landlord.

'Of course.'

'Then cycle up to the lock and alert the police.'

'At Corbeil or at Cesson?'

'It doesn't matter!'

Maigret observed Basso, feeling a little troubled. He took the revolver: only one bullet had been fired.

It was a woman's revolver, pretty, like a piece of jewellery. The bullets were tiny, nickel-plated. Yet it had only taken one to end the life of the haberdasher.

There was hardly any blood. A reddish stain on his summer jacket. Otherwise, he was as neat and tidy as usual.

'Mado has taken a turn, back in the house!' a young man cried out.

Mado was Madame Feinstein, whom they had laid on the innkeeper's tall bed. Everyone was watching Maigret. He felt a chill when a voice called out from the riverbank:

'Cooeey! . . . Where are you?'

It was Pierrot, Basso's son, who was getting out of a canoe and was looking for the group.

'Quickly! Don't let him come round!'

Marcel Basso was gathering himself together. He uncovered his face and stood up, confused by his recent show of weakness, and once again seemed to look for the person to whom he should be speaking.

'I'm a policeman,' Maigret told him.

'You know . . . It wasn't me . . .'

'Would you care to follow me?'

The inspector spoke to the doctor:

'I'm relying on you to make sure no one touches the body. And I would like to ask the rest of you to leave me and Monsieur Basso alone.'

The whole scene had been dragged out like a slow, badly directed play in the bright glare and oppressive atmosphere of the afternoon.

Some anglers passed by on the towpath, their catches

in baskets slung over their shoulders. Basso walked by Maigret's side.

'I just can't believe it . . .'

There was no spring in his step. When they turned the corner of the lean-to they saw the river, the villa on the opposite bank and Madame Basso rearranging the wicker chairs that had been left out in the garden.

'Mummy wants the key to the cellar,' the little boy shouted from his canoe.

But the man didn't reply. His expression changed to that of a hunted animal.

'Tell him where the key is.'

He summoned up his strength and called out:

'Hanging on a hook in the garage!'

'What's that?'

'On a hook in the garage!'

And his words echoed faintly:

'. . . rage!'

'What happened between you?' asked Maigret as they went inside the lean-to with the mechanical piano, empty but for the glasses left on the tables.

'I don't know . . .'

'Whose revolver is it?'

'It's not mine! . . . Mine is still in my car.'

'Did Feinstein attack you?'

A long silence. Then he sighed.

'I don't know! I didn't do anything! . . . I . . . I swear I didn't kill him.'

'You were holding the gun when . . .'

'I know . . . I don't know how that happened . . .'

'Are you saying someone else pulled the trigger?'

'No . . . I . . . You don't know how awful this is for me . . .'

'Did Feinstein kill himself?'

'He . . .'

He sat down on a bench and put his head in his hands once more. He grabbed an unfinished drink from the table and swallowed it in one go, with a grimace.

'What happens next? Are you going to arrest me?'

He stared at Maigret, his brow furrowed:

'But how did you happen to be there? You couldn't have known . . .'

He was struggling to make sense of everything, to tie together his tattered thoughts. He grimaced.

'It's like some sort of trap . . .'

The white canoe was on its way back from the far bank.

'Papa! . . . The key isn't in the garage! . . . Mummy wants to know . . .'

Mechanically, Basso felt his pockets. There was a tinkle of metal. He took out his keys and placed them on the table. Maigret took them across to the towpath and called out to the boy:

'Here! . . . Catch!'

'Thank you, monsieur.'

The canoe moved off again. Madame Basso was laying the table for dinner with the help of the maid. Some of the canoes were heading back towards the Vieux-Garçon. The landlord was cycling back from the lock, where he had made the phone call.

'Are you sure it wasn't you that pulled the trigger?'

Basso shrugged, gave a sigh and didn't reply.

The canoe reached the far bank. They could just make out the child and his mother talking. The maid was sent to fetch something inside the house, and returned almost immediately. Madame Basso took the binoculars from her and trained them on the Two-Penny Bar.

James was sitting in a corner with the landlord and his family, pouring out large glasses of brandy and stroking the cat that had nestled in his lap.

4. Meetings in Rue Royale

It had been a dreary, tiring week, full of boring chores, time-consuming tasks and countless petty frustrations. Paris remained oppressive, and around six every evening heavy thunderstorms would turn the streets into rivers.

Madame Maigret wrote from her holiday: '*The weather's lovely, I've never seen such a crop of sloes . . .*'

Maigret didn't like being in Paris without his wife. He ate without appetite in whichever restaurant was nearest to hand; he even stayed over in hotels so as not to go back home alone.

The story had all begun in the sun-filled shop on Boulevard Saint-Michel, where Basso was trying on a top hat. Then came the secret rendezvous in a furnished block in the Avenue Niel. A wedding party in the evening at the Two-Penny Bar. A game of bridge and the unexpected drama . . .

When the police had arrived on the scene, Maigret, who was off duty, left them to do their job. They had arrested the coal merchant. The prosecutor's office had been informed.

One hour later, Monsieur Basso was sitting between two police sergeants in the little railway station at Seine-Port. The Sunday crowd were all waiting for the train. The sergeant on the right offered him a cigarette.

The lamps had been lit. Night had virtually fallen. When the train had arrived in the station and everyone was crowding to get on, Basso shook off his captors, bustled his way through the crowd, ran across the rails and made for the woods on the other side.

The policemen couldn't believe their eyes. Only a few moments earlier he had been sitting there quite calm and apparently docile between the pair of them.

Maigret heard about the escape when he got back to Paris. It was an unpleasant night for everyone. The police searched the countryside around Morsang and Seine-Port, set up roadblocks, kept the railway stations under surveillance and questioned passing motorists. The net spread out over nearly the whole *département*, and weekend ramblers returning home from their walks were astonished to find the gates of Paris manned by police.

Two policemen stood guard outside the Bassos' house in Quai d'Austerlitz; two more in front of the block where the Feinsteins had their private apartment in Boulevard des Batignolles.

On Monday morning Maigret had to go to the Two-Penny Bar with magistrates from the prosecutor's office and got caught up in endless discussions.

By Monday evening, nothing! It was almost certain that Basso had slipped through the cordon and taken refuge in Paris or one of the surrounding towns, like Melun, Corbeil or Fontainebleau.

On Tuesday morning came the forensic report: a bullet fired from a distance of about thirty centimetres. It was impossible to determine whether the shot had been fired by Feinstein himself or by Basso.

Madame Feinstein identified the weapon as belonging to her. She was unaware that her husband had been carrying it in his pocket. Normally the revolver was kept – loaded – in the young woman's bedroom.

She was questioned at her flat in Boulevard des Batignolles. Unremarkable décor, few luxuries, very plain. And none too clean either – one maid to do everything.

And Madame Feinstein wept! She wept and wept! It was more or less her only response, apart from the odd 'If only I'd known!'

She had been Basso's mistress for a few months. She loved him!

'Had you had other lovers before him?'

'Monsieur!'

Of course she'd had other lovers. Feinstein couldn't have kept a live wire like her satisfied.

'How long have you been married?'

'Eight years.'

'Did your husband know about your affair?'

'Oh, no!'

'Didn't he suspect a little?'

'Not at all.'

'Do you think he would have been capable of threatening Basso with the gun if he had found out something?'

'I don't know . . . He was a strange man, very closed in on himself.'

Obviously theirs was not a marriage based on great

intimacy. Feinstein occupied with running his business, Mado left to her shopping and her secret liaisons.

And Maigret glumly pursued his investigation, proceeding by the book, questioning the concierge, the suppliers and the manager at Feinstein's shop in Boulevard des Capucines.

The case was depressing in its banality, though there was something about it that didn't feel quite right.

Feinstein had started off with a small haberdasher's on Avenue de Clichy. Then, one year after he got married, he took over a larger concern on the Boulevards, with the help of a bank loan.

From then on it was the age-old story of a small business overstretching itself: unpaid bills, bounced cheques, loans and beating the wolf from the door at the end of the month.

Nothing shady, nothing improper, but nothing solid either.

At home too they owed money to all the local tradesmen.

In the dead man's office behind his shop Maigret spent a good two hours going through his books. He found nothing unusual around the time of the crime Jean Lenoir had talked about the day before his execution.

No large receipts, no out-of-the-ordinary expenses.

Absolutely nothing, a complete blank. The investigation was grinding to a halt.

The most annoying part of it was questioning Madame Basso at Morsang. The inspector was surprised by her attitude. Although clearly sad, she was hardly in despair.

She showed a dignity of which Maigret would not have thought her capable.

'My husband must have had a good reason to run away.'

'You don't think he's guilty?'

'No.'

'But he still ran away . . . Have you heard any word from him at all?'

'No.'

'How much money did he have on him?'

'Not more than ten francs!'

The coal merchant's affairs were the exact opposite of the haberdasher's. The business never made less than 500,000 francs, even in a bad year. The offices and the yard were well organized. There were three barges moored at the quayside. Marcel Basso had inherited the business from his father and had expanded it.

Nor did the weather do much for Maigret's mood. Like all large people he suffered from the heat, and Paris wilted under the hot sun every day until three in the afternoon.

That's when the sky clouded over, the air crackled with electricity and the wind began to gust, suddenly raising swirling plumes of dust from the streets.

By late afternoon it broke: rumbles of thunder, then a deluge of rain pounding the asphalt, seeping through the awnings of the café terraces, forcing people to seek shelter in doorways.

It was on Wednesday that Maigret, caught in a sudden shower, sought shelter in the Taverne Royale. A man stood up and offered him his hand. It was James, who had been sitting alone at a table, nursing a Pernod.

The inspector hadn't seen him before in his weekday clothes. He looked more like a bank clerk now than when he was all dressed up at Morsang, but he still somehow had the air of a circus performer.

'Care for a drink?'

Maigret was exhausted. There would be a couple of hours of rain to sit out. Then he would have to go back to the Quai des Orfèvres to catch up with any news.

'A Pernod?'

Normally he only drank beer. But he didn't raise any protest. He drank mechanically. James wasn't a bad companion, and he had one salient quality: he didn't talk much!

He sat there in his cane armchair with his legs crossed, smoking cigarettes and watching the people scuttling past in the rain.

When a paper boy came by, he bought an evening paper, flicked through it vaguely, then handed it to Maigret, indicating a paragraph with his finger.

Marcel Basso, the murderer of the haberdasher from Boulevard des Capucines, is still at large, despite an extensive search by the police.

'What's your opinion?' Maigret asked.

James shrugged his shoulders, made a gesture of indifference.

'Do you think he's gone abroad?'

'I don't think he'll have gone far . . . He's probably lying low in Paris.'

'Why do you say that?'

'I don't know. I think . . . he must have had a reason for running away . . . Waiter, two more Pernods!'

Maigret had three glasses and slipped gently into a state he wasn't familiar with. He wasn't drunk, but he wasn't totally clear in the head either.

He felt agreeably mellow, sitting there on the terrace. He was able to think about the case in a more relaxed manner, almost with a degree of pleasure.

James talked about this and that, without any hint of urgency. At eight o'clock on the dot he stood up and announced:

'Time to go! My wife will be expecting me . . .'

Maigret was a little annoyed with himself for the time he'd wasted and for allowing himself to drink too much. He had dinner, then went back to his office. Neither the local police nor the Paris force had anything to report.

The next day – Thursday – he plodded on with the inquiry with the same lack of enthusiasm.

He waded through files dating back ten years but found nothing relating to the information Jean Lenoir had given.

He looked through the legal registers. He rang around the hospitals and sanatoriums in the vague hope of finding Victor, Lenoir's friend with tuberculosis.

There were lots of Victors, but not the right one!

By midday, Maigret had a splitting head but no appetite. He had lunch in Place Dauphin, in a little restaurant popular with police officers. Then he phoned Morsang, where policemen had been posted outside the Bassos' villa.

No sign. Madame Basso was carrying on with life as

normal with her son. She read all the papers. The villa didn't have a telephone.

At five o'clock, Maigret came out of the apartment block on the Avenue Niel. He had come on the off chance of digging something up, but hadn't found anything.

Then mechanically, as if he'd already been doing it for years, he headed off to the Taverne Royale, where he was greeted by James, and sat down beside him.

'What's new?' James asked him, then before he could answer called out: 'Two Pernods!'

The storm was behind schedule today. The streets remained bathed in sunlight. Coachloads of tourists drove past.

'The most straightforward hypothesis,' Maigret murmured, as if to himself, 'the one the newspapers seem to favour, is that Basso was attacked by his companion for some reason or another, grabbed hold of the gun that was pointed at him and shot the haberdasher . . .'

'Which is rubbish.'

Maigret looked at James, who also seemed to be talking to himself.

'Why do you say it's rubbish?'

'Because if Feinstein had wanted to kill Basso, he'd have been a bit more calculating than that. He was a cool customer, a skilful bridge player.'

The inspector couldn't help smiling at the serious tone in which James said this.

'So what's your theory?'

'I don't exactly have a theory. Just that Basso should never have got involved with Mado. You can tell just by looking at her that she's not the sort of woman who lets a man go easily, once she's got her claws into him.'

'Had her husband shown any signs of being jealous?'

'What, him?'

And James gave Maigret a curious look. There was an ironic twinkle in his eye.

'Don't you know?'

James shrugged his shoulders and murmured:

'It's none of my business. Besides, if he was the jealous type, then most of the Morsang gang would be dead by now.'

'You mean they were all . . . ?'

'Well, not all. Let's not exaggerate. Let's just say that Mado danced with everyone, and when you danced with Mado, you could end up disappearing into the bushes.'

'Including you?'

'I don't dance,' James replied.

'If what you say is true, then Feinstein must have known.'

The Englishman sighed.

'I don't know! But he did owe all of them money.'

At first sight, James came across as a drunken oaf. But there was a lot more to him than met the eye.

Maigret whistled.

'Well, well.'

'Two Pernods! Two!

'Yes. Mado didn't even have to know. It was all very discreet. Feinstein tapped his wife's lovers for money, without letting on that he knew, but leaving the implication hanging in the air . . .'

They didn't talk much after that. The storm still hadn't

broken. Maigret drank his Pernods, his eyes fixed on the crowds flowing past in the street outside. He was comfortably ensconced in his chair, turning over in his mind this new complexion on the case.

'Eight o'clock! . . .'

James shook his hand and set off, just at the moment the storm was beginning to break.

By Friday it had become a daily habit. Maigret headed for the Taverne Royale almost without realizing it. At one point, he couldn't resist asking:

'Don't you ever go home after work? Between five and eight you seem to . . .'

'You have to have a little bolt-hole to call your own,' James sighed.

And James's bolt-hole was a café terrace, a marble-topped table, a cloudy aperitif; his view was the columns of the Madeleine, the waiters' white aprons and the crowds and traffic in the street.

'How long have you been married?'

'Eight years.'

Maigret didn't dare ask him whether he loved his wife. In any case, James would probably say yes. Only after eight o'clock! After the bolt-hole!

Maigret wondered whether they were starting to become friends.

Today they didn't discuss the case. Maigret drank his three Pernods. He needed to blot out the hard day he'd had. His life was clogged up with trivial problems.

It was the holidays, and he was having to fill in for several absent colleagues. And the examining magistrate in the Two-Penny Bar case never gave him a moment's peace. He had sent him to interrogate Mado Feinstein for a second time, told him to examine the haberdasher's books and to question Basso's employees.

The police were already short-handed, and a number of officers were pinned down watching the places where the fugitive was likely to show up. This all put the chief in a bad mood.

'Haven't you got this one sorted out yet?' he had asked that morning.

Maigret agreed with James. He sensed that Basso was in Paris. But how had he been able to get hold of money? And if he hadn't, how was he living? What was he hoping for? What was he expecting to happen? What was he doing with himself?

His guilt had not been proven. If he had stayed in custody and hired a good lawyer he could have hoped, if not for acquittal, then at least a light sentence. After which he could return to his business, his wife and his son. Instead of that, he was running away, in hiding, and thus giving up all his former life.

'He must have his reasons,' James had said in his usual philosophical way.

Don't let us down. Will be at station. Love.

It was Saturday. Madame Maigret had sent an affectionate ultimatum. Her husband wasn't yet sure how to reply. But at five o'clock he was at the Taverne Royale, shaking James's hand. James ordered as usual:

'Pernod!'

As on the previous Saturday, there was a rush to the stations – a continuous stream of taxis piled high with luggage, the bustle of people getting away on holiday.

'Are you going to Morsang?'

'Yes, as usual.'

'It'll be a strange atmosphere.'

The inspector wanted to go to Morsang himself. On the other hand, he wanted to see his wife, to go trout fishing in the rivers of Alsace, to breathe in the lovely smells of his sister-in-law's house.

He couldn't make his mind up. He vaguely observed James get up and head to the back of the bar.

There was nothing unusual in this. He thought nothing of it and barely registered the fact that his companion returned after a few moments and sat down again.

Five, ten minutes went past. A waiter approached.

'Is one of you two gentlemen Monsieur Maigret?'

'That's me. What is it?'

'A phone call for you . . .'

Maigret stood up and went to the back of the bar, frowning; despite his inebriation, he could smell something fishy. When he went into the box, he turned round to see James looking at him from the terrace.

'Strange,' he muttered. 'Hello! . . . Hello! . . . This is Maigret . . . Who's calling? . . .'

He started to snap his fingers impatiently. Finally there was a woman's voice at the other end of the line.

'How can I help you?'

'Hello . . . who's there?'

'This is the operator. Which number do you require?'

'But you called me, mademoiselle.'

'Not so, monsieur. This number hasn't been rung for at least ten minutes. Please hang up.'

He bashed the door open with his fist. Outside, in the shade of the terrace, there was a man standing next to James. It was Marcel Basso. He looked different in new, ill-fitting clothes. He was keeping an anxious eye on the door of the phone box.

He saw Maigret at the same moment the latter spotted him. Maigret saw his lips move – a few quick words – then he dashed off into the crowds outside.

'How many calls?' the cashier asked the inspector.

But Maigret was running. The terrace was crowded, he had to weave his way through, and by the time he reached the street there was no way of knowing in which direction Basso had fled. There were dozens of taxis out on the street – had he hopped into one of them? Or even leaped on to a passing bus? . . .

Maigret returned to his table, scowling. He sat down without a word, without looking at James, who hadn't moved a muscle. A waiter approached.

'The cashier would like to know how many calls you made.'

'Damn!'

He noticed a smile on James's lips and said crossly:

'Congratulations!'

'You reckon?'

'How long did it take you to hatch this little scheme?'

'It was pretty much off the cuff. Waiter, two Pernods! And some cigarettes!'

'What did he say to you? What did he want?'

James leaned back in his chair and merely sighed, as if he couldn't see the point of this conversation.

'Money? And where did he get hold of that suit he was wearing?'

'He can't be expected to walk round Paris in white flannels!'

That was indeed what Basso was wearing when he ran away at Seine-Port station. James forgot nothing.

'Have you contacted him prior to today?'

'He contacted me!'

'And you have nothing to say?'

'You'd do the same as me. I've been a guest at his house hundreds of times. He's never done me any harm!'

'Did he want money?'

'He's been watching us for half an hour. I thought I saw him yesterday across the road. He just didn't dare come over.'

'So you had me summoned to the phone.'

'He seemed tired.'

'Did he say anything?'

'It's weird how different clothes can change a man . . .' James sighed, evading the question.

Maigret observed him out of the corner of his eye.

'Are you aware that, by rights, you could be arrested for aiding and abetting?'

'There are lots of things you can do by rights. But rights aren't always right.'

He was clowning around as usual.

'Waiter, where are those Pernods?'

'Coming!'

'Are you coming down to Morsang? Because if you are, we may as well get a taxi. It's only a hundred francs, and the train costs . . .'

'What about your wife?'

'She always comes by taxi, with her sister and her friends. Five of them, that works out at twenty francs a head, whereas the train costs . . .'

'OK.'

'Coming or not?'

'I'm coming. Waiter, how much is that?'

'Excuse me. Separate bills, as usual.'

It was a matter of principle. Maigret paid for his own drinks, James for his. He added ten francs for the 'phone call'.

In the taxi, James appeared preoccupied. When they reached Villejuif, he revealed what was on his mind:

'I wonder where we'll be playing bridge tomorrow afternoon.'

It was time for the storm. The first drops of rain began to streak the windscreen.

5. The Doctor's Car

They might have expected to find a different atmosphere at Morsang. It had only been the previous Sunday that the events had taken place. One of the group was now dead, another was a wanted murderer.

Nevertheless, when James and Maigret arrived, they found a group of people standing around a new car, admiring it. They had exchanged their weekday clothes for their sports gear. Only the doctor was still dressed in a suit.

It was his car, and he was giving it its first outing. Everyone was asking questions, and he was extolling its special features.

'Yes, it does guzzle more gas, but . . .'

Almost everyone had a car. The doctor's was brand new.

'The engine purrs, just listen to this . . .'

His wife was sitting contentedly inside the car, happy to let the confab take its course. Doctor Mertens was about thirty, skinny as a rake, as limp-wristed as a sickly young girl.

'Is that your new car?' James asked, bursting into the conversation.

He strode around it, muttering to himself inaudibly.

'I wouldn't mind taking it for a spin tomorrow. Is that all right with you?'

One would have thought that Maigret's presence would

disturb them. They hardly noticed he was there! They all felt so at home at the inn, they came and went as they pleased.

'Your wife not with you, James?'

'She's coming with Marcelle and Lili.'

They took their canoes out of the garage. Someone was repairing a fishing-rod with some silk cord. They all did their own thing until dinnertime. There wasn't much conversation during the meal, just the odd exchange here and there.

'Is Madame Basso at home?'

'What a week she must have had!'

'What are we doing tomorrow?'

Maigret was like a spare part. Everyone avoided him, without making it too obvious. When James wasn't with him, he would wander the terrace or the riverbank alone. When night fell he slipped off to check with the officers who were guarding the Bassos' villa.

There were two of them on duty. They took it in turn to take their meals in a bistro in Seine-Port, two kilometres away. When the inspector arrived, the one who was off duty was fishing.

'Anything to report?'

'Not a thing. She keeps herself to herself. Every now and again she takes a tour round the garden. The tradesmen have been calling as usual: the baker at nine, the butcher a short while later, then the greengrocer comes by with his cart around eleven.'

There was a light on on the ground floor. They could make out the silhouette of the boy drinking his soup with a serviette tied around his neck. The policemen were stationed in a little wood on the riverbank. The one who was fishing said:

'This place is teeming with rabbits. If we weren't on a job . . .'

Opposite, the Two-Penny Bar, where two couples – probably workers from Corbeil – were dancing to the strains of the mechanical piano.

A Sunday morning like any other at Morsang, with anglers all along the banks, others sitting immobile in green-painted dinghies anchored at both ends, canoes, a couple of sailing-boats.

It was a well-ordered routine that nothing was going to disrupt.

The countryside was pretty, the sky was clear, everyone was at peace. Perhaps that's why the scene was as sickly as an overly sweet dessert.

Maigret found James dressed in a blue-and-white-striped sweater, white trousers and espadrilles, with an American sailing cap perched on his head. He was sipping a large glass of brandy and water by way of breakfast.

'Did you sleep well?'

Maigret noticed one amusing detail: in Paris, he always addressed Maigret with the formal *vous*. Here in Morsang, he used the familiar *tu* for everyone, including the inspector, without even realizing.

'What are you up to this morning?'

'I think I'll drop in on the Two-Penny Bar.'

'I'll see you there. Apparently we've arranged a get-together there for pre-lunch drinks. Do you want to borrow a canoe?'

Maigret was the only one in dark city clothes. He was given a small flat-bottomed boat which he had great trouble keeping steady. When he arrived at the Two-Penny Bar, it was ten o'clock in the morning, and there wasn't a customer in sight.

Or rather, there was one, in the kitchen munching on a hunk of bread and a fat sausage. The old woman was saying to him:

'You want to take better care. One of my lads didn't look after himself properly and it killed him. And he was bigger and stronger than you!'

At that moment the customer had a coughing fit and couldn't swallow his mouthful of bread. As he was coughing, he noticed Maigret standing at the door and he frowned.

'A bottle of beer!' said the inspector.

'Wouldn't you prefer to sit out on the terrace?'

No, he preferred the kitchen, with its table scored by knife marks, its rush chairs and its stove on which a large pot was bubbling away.

'My son has gone off to Corbeil to chase up some bottles of soda water they forgot to deliver. Would you help me open the trapdoor?'

The trapdoor in the middle of the kitchen was opened to reveal the gaping hole of a damp cellar. The stooping old woman went down into it while the customer never took his eyes off Maigret.

He was a pale, thin young man of about twenty-five with blond stubble on his cheeks. He had deep-set eyes and thin, colourless lips.

But what was most striking about him was what he was wearing. He wasn't dressed in rags, like a vagabond. Nor did he have that insolent look of the professional tramp.

No, he displayed a strange mixture of shyness and self-confidence. He was humble and aggressive at the same time. He was both clean and dirty.

His clothes were neat and well kept, even though he looked as if he had been on the road for days.

'Show me your papers, please.'

Maigret had no need to identify himself as a policeman. The boy had grasped that straight away. He took a grubby army identity card from his pocket. The inspector read the name under his breath:

'Victor Gaillard!'

He calmly closed the card and returned it to its owner. The old woman came back up from the cellar and closed the trapdoor.

'Nice and cold,' she said, opening the bottle of beer.

And she went back to peeling potatoes while the two men began talking in a steady, dispassionate tone.

'Last address?'

'The municipal sanatorium in Gien.'

'When did you leave?'

'A month ago.'

'And since then?'

'I've been broke, on the road. You could arrest me for

vagrancy, but they'd just put me back in a sanatorium. I've only got one lung left.'

There was nothing self-pitying in his tone. On the contrary, it was as if he were presenting his credentials.

'Did you get a letter from Lenoir?'

'Who's Lenoir?'

'Stop messing about. He told you you'd find your man at the Two-Penny Bar.'

'I'd had enough of the sanatorium.'

'And thought you'd squeeze a bit more out of the guy from the Canal Saint-Martin!'

The old woman listened without understanding, without showing any surprise. It was as if they were having an everyday conversation in this rundown country kitchen, where a hen had wandered in and was pecking away around their feet.

'Have you got nothing to say?'

'I don't know what you're talking about.'

'Lenoir told me everything.'

'I don't know any Lenoir.'

Maigret shrugged his shoulders, lit his pipe and repeated:

'Stop messing about! You know I know what you're up to.'

'What's the worst they can do? Send me back to the sanatorium.'

'I know, I know . . . you've only got one lung.'

Some canoes glided past on the river.

'What Lenoir told you is true. Your man is here.'

'I'm not saying anything.'

'So much the worse for you. If you haven't changed

your mind by this evening, I'll have you locked up for vagrancy. After that, we'll see . . .'

Maigret looked him in the eye. He could read him like a book. He'd met his sort before.

A different kettle of fish entirely from Lenoir. Victor was the sort who rode on the back of the bigger villains, the one who's always put on lookout duty and gets the smallest share of the loot.

He was one of those types who is easily led astray and doesn't have the strength of character to get back on the rails. He had started hanging around the streets and the dance halls at the age of sixteen. With Lenoir, he had landed on his feet that night at the Canal Saint-Martin, and had managed to live off the proceeds of his blackmail as if it were a regular salary.

But for his tuberculosis, he would probably have become a stooge in Lenoir's gang. But his ill health meant he ended up in the sanatorium. He must have driven the doctors and nurses to despair with his thieving and petty misdemeanours. Maigret guessed that he had faced the courts on more than one occasion and had been in and out of various sanatoriums, hospitals, hospices and young offenders' institutions.

He wasn't afraid. He had the same answer to everything: his lung. He'd be living off it until the day it killed him.

'What do I care?'

'Are you refusing to tell me the name of the man at the Canal?'

'Don't know what you're talking about.'

There was an ironic twinkle in his eyes as he said this. He bit off a large chunk of sausage and started chewing it assiduously.

'I know Lenoir wouldn't have said anything,' he murmured, after a pensive pause. 'Not like that, right at the end . . .'

Maigret stayed cool. He knew he had the upper hand. What's more, he now had a new means of getting to the truth.

'Another beer, please, madame.'

'A good thing I brought three bottles up.'

She gave Victor a curious look, as if trying to work out what crime he could have committed.

'To think you were well taken care of in the sanatorium and you left. Just like my son! He'd rather have his freedom than . . .'

Maigret watched the canoes row past in the bright sunlight outside. It was nearly time for drinks. A sailing-boat containing James's wife and two of her friends pulled in at the riverbank outside. The three women beckoned to a canoe, which followed close behind. Other boats followed. The old woman sighed:

'My son hasn't got back yet. I won't be able to manage on my own. My daughter has gone to fetch the milk.'

Nevertheless, she gathered up some glasses, which she took out to the tables on the terrace, then she dug some loose change out of a pocket concealed under her petticoat.

'They'll need some pennies for the piano.'

Maigret stayed where he was, one eye on the new

arrivals and the other on his sickly companion, who continued to munch away unperturbed. And he noticed the Bassos' villa in the background, with its blooming garden, its diving-board next to the river, its two boats moored at the bank, the child's swing.

He gave a sudden start when he heard what sounded like a shot being fired in the distance. The people next to the river looked up too. But there was nothing to be seen. Nothing happened. Ten minutes went by. The guests from the Vieux-Garçon took their seats around the tables. The old woman came out, carrying several bottles of aperitif.

Then a dark figure ran down the Bassos' lawn. Maigret recognized one of the police officers. He fumbled with the chain of one of the boats, got in and started rowing towards them with all his might.

Maigret stood up and turned to Victor.

'You . . . stay put.'

'Happy to oblige.'

Outside, everyone had stopped ordering drinks, intent on the sight of the officer rowing across. Maigret walked down to the reeds by the river and waited impatiently.

'What's happened?'

The officer was out of breath.

'Get in . . . I swear it wasn't my fault.'

With Maigret on board, he started rowing back across to the villa.

'It was all quiet. The greengrocer had just been round. Madame Basso was walking in the garden with the child. I don't know why, I just had this feeling something was up – like they were expecting something. Then a car pulled up, a brand-new car. It parked just outside the gate, and a man got out.'

'Balding, in his thirties?'

'That's right! He came into the garden and started walking with Madame Basso and the boy. You know where my observation post is . . . it's a fair distance away. They shook hands. The woman walked the man back to the gate. He climbed in and turned on the ignition. And before I could make a move, Madame Basso jumped in with the boy, and the car sped off.'

'Who fired the shot?'

'I did. I was trying to puncture a tyre.'

'Was Berger with you?'

'Yes. I sent him to Seine-Port to phone around everyone.'

This was the second time they'd had to alert all the police stations in Seine-et-Oise. The boat reached the far bank. Maigret went into the garden. But what could they do there now? There was nothing to do but phone around and alert the other stations.

Maigret bent over to pick up a woman's handkerchief, embroidered with Madame Basso's initials. She had pulled it to ribbons as she had nervously waited for James to appear.

What upset the inspector the most was the thought of all those hours he had whiled away drinking Pernod with the Englishman on the terrace of the Taverne Royale. Now he resented that. He was annoyed that he had let down his guard and allowed himself to be sucked in.

'Shall I carry on keeping an eye on the villa?'

'In case the bricks run off? No, go and find Berger. Then the two of you help with the search. Try and get hold of a motorbike, and bring me hourly updates.'

On the kitchen table, next to the vegetables, there was an envelope bearing James's writing:

To be delivered without fail to Madame Basso.

Obviously the greengrocer had delivered the letter. It told the young woman what was going to happen. That's why she was nervously patrolling the garden with her son.

Maigret rowed back to the Two-Penny Bar. He found the group gathered round the vagrant. Someone had given him an aperitif, and the doctor was asking him questions. Victor had the cheek to give the inspector a look as if to say:

'I'm busy. Leave me alone . . .'

And he continued with his explanation:

'He was an important professor, apparently. They filled my lung with oxygen, right, and then they sealed it like a balloon . . .'

The doctor smiled at the way he described it, but nodded to his companions to show that what he was saying was true.

'Now they have to do the same thing with the half-lung on the other side, because you've got two lungs, see, or in my case one and a half.'

'And you drink alcohol?'

'Yeah. Cheers.'

'Do you get cold sweats at night?'

'Sometimes. When I sleep in draughty barns.'

'What are you drinking, inspector?' someone asked. 'Has something happened that they had to come and fetch you like that?'

'Tell me, doctor, did James borrow your car this morning?'

'He asked if he could take it for a spin. He'll be back soon . . .'

'I very much doubt it.'

The doctor gave a start, then tried to smile as he stammered:

'You're joking, of course . . .'

'I assure you I'm quite serious. He's just used it to abduct Madame Basso and her son.'

'What . . . James?' the doctor's wife asked, unable to believe her ears.

'Yes, James.'

'It must have been a joke. He really likes a good hoax.'

Victor was greatly amused by this. He sipped his drink and looked at Maigret with a sardonic smile.

The landlord returned from Corbeil in his little pony and trap. As he was unloading the bottles of soda water, he happened to say:

'What a palaver! You can't go down the road now without being stopped by the police. Luckily they know who I am.'

'Was this on the road to Corbeil?'

'Yes, just a few minutes ago. There are ten of them next to the bridge. They're stopping cars and asking everyone to show their papers. So there's a tailback of about thirty cars.'

Maigret turned away. It was nothing to do with him. It had to be done, but it was an extremely crude and heavy-handed method. And it was a lot for people to put up with two Sundays in a row, in the same *département*, especially for a small-scale crime that had had very little coverage in the newspapers.

Had he lost track of the case? Had he been left floundering in the wake of events? Once again the memory of the hours spent drinking with James in the Taverne Royale came back to haunt him.

'What are you drinking?' he heard a voice ask. 'A large Pernod?'

The very word was enough to remind him of the week gone by, the Sunday get-togethers of the Morsang crowd, the whole disagreeable case.

'A beer,' he replied.

'At this hour?'

The well-meaning waiter who had offered him the aperitif was taken aback at the fury of Maigret's response:

'Yes, at this hour!'

Victor, too, received a bad-tempered look. The doctor was talking about him to the fishermen:

'I've heard of the treatment, but I've never seen such a thoroughgoing application of the technique of pneumothorax . . .'

Then, in a whisper:

'Not that it'll make much difference. I'd give him a year at most . . .'

★

Maigret had lunch at the Vieux-Garçon, ensconced in a corner like a wounded beast, growling if anyone came near. Twice the police officer came on his motorbike to report in.

'Nothing. The car was spotted on the road to Fontainebleau, but hasn't been seen since.'

Marvellous! A traffic jam on the Fontainebleau road! Hundreds of cars held up!

Two hours later, it was reported that a car matching the description of the doctor's car had filled up at a petrol station at Arpajon. But was it the right one? The petrol-pump attendant had sworn there was no woman in the car.

Finally, at five o'clock, a message from Montlhéry. The car had been seen doing circuits of the racetrack, as if on a time trial, when it blew a tyre. By sheer chance a policeman had asked the driver for his licence. He didn't have one.

It was James, and he was on his own. They were waiting for Maigret's instructions whether to let him go or lock him up.

'They were brand-new tyres,' the doctor moaned. 'And on its first time out! I'm beginning to think he's mad. Or else he's drunk, as usual.'

And he asked Maigret if he could come with him.

6. Haggling

They made a detour to the Two-Penny Bar to pick up Victor. Once he was in the car, he turned and gave the landlord a look which meant something like 'You see the special treatment I'm getting?'

He was sitting on the fold-down seat, facing Maigret. The window was wound down, and he had the impudence to ask:

'Do you mind if I close it? It's because of my lung, you know.'

At the track there were no races on today. There were a few drivers doing practice laps in front of the empty stands. The emptiness of the place, if anything, made it seem more vast.

A short distance away, a parked car; a police officer was standing next to a man in a leather helmet who was on his knees tinkering with his bike.

'Over there,' the inspector was told.

Victor was fascinated by a racing-car hurtling round the track at around 200 kilometres an hour. Now he opened the window so he could lean out to get a better view.

'It's my car all right,' said the doctor. 'I hope it isn't damaged . . .'

Then they saw James, standing quite calmly next to the motorcyclist, stroking his chin, giving advice on how to fix the engine. When he saw Maigret and his companions approach, he murmured:

'That was quick!'

Then he looked at Victor from head to toe, as if wondering what he was doing there.

'Who's this?'

If Maigret had been hoping for something from this meeting, he was disappointed. Victor scarcely noticed the Englishman, he was too interested in watching the racing-car. The doctor was already inspecting the inside of his car for any signs of damage.

'Have you been here long?' the inspector growled.

'I'm not sure . . . quite long, yes.'

He was so self-possessed, it was unbelievable. You wouldn't think to look at him that he had just whisked away a woman and her child from under the noses of the police, and because of him the entire Seine-et-Oise force was on a state of alert.

'Don't worry,' he said to the doctor. 'Nothing worse than a puncture. The rest of the car is intact. It's a good machine . . . the clutch is a little sticky, perhaps . . .'

'Did Basso ask you yesterday to pick up his wife and child?'

'You know very well I can't answer questions like that, my dear Maigret.'

'And I don't suppose you will tell me where you dropped them off?'

'I'm sure if you were in my shoes . . .'

'I'll give you credit for one thing, something even a professional criminal wouldn't have thought of.'

James was modestly surprised.

'What's that?'

'The racetrack. Having delivered Madame Basso safely, you didn't want the police to find the car straight away. And since there were roadblocks everywhere, you thought of the racetrack. You could have driven round and round for hours.'

'I'd always fancied having a go at it, you know.'

But the inspector wasn't listening. He dashed over to the doctor, who was attempting to fit the spare tyre.

'I'm sorry, the car stays put until we receive the order to release it.'

'What? But this is *my* car! I haven't done anything . . .'

It was no use protesting. The car was put into a lock-up, and Maigret took away the key. The policeman awaited instructions. James smoked a cigarette. Victor was still watching the racing-cars.

'Take him away,' said Maigret, indicating Victor, 'and put him in a cell.'

'What about me?' James asked.

'Do you still have nothing to say to me?'

'Not really. Put yourself in my shoes!'

Maigret sulkily turned his back on him.

Maigret was delighted when it began to rain on the Monday. The grey weather chimed in better with his mood and the tedious tasks of the day.

Among them, he had to write a report on the events of the day before, in which he had to justify his deployment of the officers under his command.

At eleven o'clock, two officers from Criminal Records

came to collect him from his office, and all three of them took a taxi to the racetrack, where Maigret was able to do little except watch his colleagues at work.

They knew that the doctor had clocked up only sixty kilometres since buying the car. The dial now showed 210 kilometres. They reckoned that James must have done about fifty kilometres at the racetrack.

That left about a hundred kilometres to account for. The distance between Morsang and Montlhéry was barely forty kilometres by the most direct route.

Using this information, they were able to mark a circle on a route map showing the maximum area the car could have reached.

The two experts worked meticulously. They carefully scraped the tyres, gathered up the dust and other debris and examined it under a magnifying glass, putting some of it aside for further analysis.

'Fresh tar,' one of them said.

And the other examined a special map provided by the transport department, looking for places within their circle where there were current roadworks. There were four or five, all in different directions. The first expert said:

'Chalk deposits.'

Now they consulted a military map. Maigret walked up and down glumly, smoking his pipe.

'No calcareous soil in the Fontainebleau area, but between La Ferté-Allais and Arpajon . . .'

'I've found some grains of wheat in the tread . . .'

And so the evidence accumulated. The maps became covered in blue and red lines.

At two o'clock they rang the town hall at La Ferté-Allais to find out whether any firm in the town was currently using Portland cement in such a way that some of it could have found its way on to the road. They didn't get their answer until three o'clock:

'There's building work going on at the Essonne mills. There's cement on the main road from La Ferté to Arpajon.'

They had pinned down one thing. The car had definitely passed through there. The experts took away a few other objects to examine more closely in the laboratory.

Maigret checked off all the towns and villages within the circle on the map, and rang round the relevant police stations and municipal offices.

At four o'clock, he left his office intending to interrogate Victor, whom he had not seen since the previous day and who was now held in the temporary cell at the foot of the stairs at the police headquarters. As he descended the stairs, however, he had an idea. He returned to his office and telephoned the accountant of Basso's firm.

'Hello! Police! Could you tell me the name of your bank? . . . The Banque du Nord, Boulevard Haussmann. Thank you.'

He had himself driven to the bank, where he asked to see the manager. Five minutes later, Maigret had another lead in his inquiry. At ten o'clock that morning, James had cashed a cheque for 300,000 francs drawn up by Marcel Basso.

The cheque was dated four days previously.

*

'Boss, the guy downstairs wants to see you. Says he has something important to tell you.'

Maigret walked ponderously downstairs and entered the cell, where Victor was sitting on a bench, leaning on the table with his head in his hands.

'I'm listening.'

The prisoner stood up briskly. He had a cunning look on his face. Shifting from one foot to the other, he said:

'You haven't found anything yet, have you?'

'Still pursuing our inquiries.'

'See, you haven't found anything yet. I'm not stupid . . . Anyway, last night I had a bit of a think.'

'You've decided to talk?'

'Hold on! We need to reach an understanding. I don't know if Lenoir talked or not. If he did, he didn't tell you everything. Without me, you won't get anywhere. That's a fact. You're stuck, and you're going to stay that way. So, this is what I've got to say. Information like that's got to be worth something. Got to be worth a lot. Let's say I went and found the murderer and told him I was going to tell the police everything. Don't you think he'd cough up whatever I asked for?'

Victor had that triumphant look of the underdog who suddenly finds himself in a position of power. All his life the police had hassled him, and now he felt that he had the upper hand. He was strutting around looking very pleased with himself.

'So there it is. Why would I talk? Why would I harm someone who hasn't done me any wrong? You think you can put me away for vagrancy? You're forgetting my lung. They'll send me to a hospital, then to a sanato-rium.'

Maigret looked at him steadily, but didn't say a word.

'How's about 30,000 francs? It's not a lot. Just enough to see me through to the end, which can't be long now. Thirty grand – what's a piddling amount like that to the government?'

He imagined he already had the money in his hands. He was exultant. He was interrupted by a coughing fit, which brought tears to his eyes, but they were like tears of triumph. Wasn't he smart? Wasn't he in the driving seat?

'That's my final offer. Thirty thousand francs and I tell you everything. You'll get your man. There'll be a promo-tion in it for you. You'll have your name in the papers. Otherwise, nothing! You can do what you like with me. Just remember, it all took place six years ago, and there were only two witnesses: Lenoir, who won't be saying any more, and yours truly . . .'

'Is that it?' asked Maigret, who had remained standing the whole time.

'You think it's too much?'

Victor felt a pang of disquiet at Maigret's calm, inscrut-able reaction.

'I'm not scared of you, you know.' He gave a forced laugh. 'I know the score. You could rough me up a bit, but I'd tell the papers how the police beat up a poor invalid with one lung . . .'

'Are you finished?'

'Don't think you'll find the truth on your own. If you ask me, 30,000 francs is not much to pay . . .'

'Are you finished?'

'And if you think I'm stupid enough to go after the guy if you let me go, you've got another think coming. I won't write to him, I won't ring him . . .'

His tone had changed now. He felt the ground slipping under him, but he was still trying to put on a brave face.

'Anyway, I want to see a lawyer. You can't keep me here more than twenty-four hours.'

Maigret blew out a little puff of smoke, thrust his hands in his pockets and left the cell. On the way out he said to the warder:

'Lock him in.'

He was angry, and now he was on his own he could let it show in his face. He was angry because he had this idiot in his grasp, at his mercy, but he couldn't get anything out of him.

And that was because he was an idiot, because he thought he was cunning and tough!

He thought he could use his lung as a form of black-mail!

Three or four times during this interview, the inspector had almost struck him across the face, to knock some sense into him, but had managed to restrain himself.

In truth, his hand was not a strong one. Legally, he had nothing on Victor.

He had plenty of previous form, for sure; he'd led his whole life going from one petty crime to the next. But there was nothing new, except a vagrancy charge, that Maigret could get him on.

And he was right about the lung. He'd have everyone

on his side. The newspapers would devote several column inches to portraying the police as monsters.

Dying man beaten by police!

So he stood there calm as you like, demanding to be paid 30,000 francs! And he was right when he said they would soon have to release him!

'Let him out tonight at around one o'clock. Tell Sergeant Lucas to follow him and not to let him out of his sight.'

And Maigret clenched his teeth round the stem of his pipe. Victor knew, and he only had to say one word. Now Maigret was stuck with having to concoct theories out of diverse, and sometimes contradictory, evidence.

He hailed a taxi and barked at the driver:

'To the Taverne Royale!'

James wasn't there. Eight o'clock came and he still hadn't turned up. The doorman at the bank confirmed that he had left at five as usual.

Maigret had a meal of *choucroute*, then phoned his office around 8.30.

'Has the prisoner asked to see me?'

'Yes. He says he's given the matter more thought and he's willing to come down to 25,000. That's his final offer. And he wants it put on the record that a man in his condition shouldn't be fed bread without butter and be forced to stay in a cell where the temperature never gets above sixteen degrees.'

Maigret put down the receiver. He went for a short walk in the Boulevards, then caught a taxi to Rue Championnet, where James lived. His block was enormous, like a barracks. It contained small apartments inhabited by office workers, commercial travellers and small investors.

'Fourth, on the left.'

There was no lift, so the inspector slowly climbed the stairs, catching a whiff of cooking or hearing children's voices from behind the doors on each landing.

James's wife answered the door. She was dressed in a pretty royal-blue dressing gown – it wasn't particularly luxurious, but it didn't look that cheap either.

'You wish to speak to my husband?'

The entrance hall was barely wider than a dining-table. On the walls were pictures of sailing-boats, bathers, young men and women in sporting garb.

'It's for you, James!'

She pushed open a door, ushered Maigret through and sat back down in her armchair next to the window, where she picked up her crochet.

The other apartments in the block were still decorated in the style of the last century, with their Henry II and Louis-Philippe furniture.

This apartment, however, felt more like Montparnasse than Montmartre. It owed more to the decorative arts in style, but seemed to be the work of an amateur.

Plywood partitions had been erected at odd angles, and most of the furniture had been removed to make way for shelving painted in bright colours.

The carpet was in a single colour, a rather lurid green.

The lampshades were meant to resemble parchment.

It all looked smart and fresh, but seemed to lack solidity; you felt that the walls might give way if you leaned on them and that the paintwork was not quite dry.

Above all, especially when James stood up, you felt that the apartment was too small for him, that he was boxed in and had to be careful not to bash into things when he moved around.

An open door to the right revealed the bathroom, where there was only just enough space for the bath. The kitchen was no more than a galley, with a spirit stove on a bench.

James was sitting in a small chair with a cigarette in his mouth and a book in his hands.

Maigret had the distinct impression that there was no contact at all between these two people.

They each sat in their own corner, James reading, his wife crocheting, with only the sound of the cars and trams outside the window to break the silence.

No hint of intimacy whatsoever.

He stood up, offered Maigret his hand, smiling awkwardly, as though he were embarrassed to be seen in such a place.

'How are you, Maigret?'

But his familiar cordiality had a different ring in this doll's house of an apartment. It seemed to clash with the furnishings, the carpet, the modern ornaments arranged on the shelves, the wallpaper, the fancy lampshades . . .

'I'm fine, thank you.'

'Take a seat. I was just reading an English novel.'

And his expression was saying:

'Don't mind all this. It's none of my doing. I don't feel at home here.'

His wife listened in, without interrupting her work.

'Do we have anything to drink, Marthe?' he asked her.

'You know we don't!'

Then to the inspector:

'It's his fault. If we ever get any bottles of liquor in, they get drunk within a couple of days. He has enough to drink when he's out.'

'Inspector, what do you say we go down to the bistro?'

But before Maigret could respond, James frowned as he looked at his wife, who must have been making urgent signals to him.

'If you'd like to . . .'

He closed his book with a sigh and started fidgeting with a paperweight lying on a low table next to him.

The room was not more than four metres long, and yet it felt like two rooms, as if two people lived their lives here without ever crossing each other's path.

The wife, who had decorated the flat entirely to her own taste, spent her time sewing, embroidering, cooking, making dresses, while James would come home every evening at eight and eat his dinner without saying a word, then read until bedtime, when that sofa covered with brightly coloured cushions was pulled out to form a bed.

It was easier now to understand James's need for his 'little bolt-hole' on the terrace of the Taverne Royale, with his glass of Pernod in front of him.

'Sure. Let's go.'

And James leaped to his feet with a sigh of relief.

'Could you wait a moment while I get my shoes?'

He was wearing slippers. He squeezed between the bath and the wall. The bathroom door was still open, but his wife didn't bother lowering her voice:

'Don't pay any attention. He's not like other people.' And she started counting her stitches: 'Seven . . . eight . . . nine . . . Do you think he knows something about the business at Morsang?'

'Where is the shoehorn?' James muttered as he rummaged noisily through a cupboard.

She looked at Maigret as if to say 'You see what I mean?'

James finally emerged from the bathroom, once more looking too large for the room, and said to his wife:

'I'll be back soon.'

'I've heard that before.'

He motioned to the inspector to get a move on, no doubt fearing his wife might change her mind. Even in the stairwell he seemed too big, as if he didn't match the décor.

The first building on the left was a bar frequented by taxi drivers.

'It's the only one around here.'

The dim lighting glinted off the zinc counter. There were four men playing cards at the back of the bar.

'Ah, Monsieur James, the usual?' said the landlord, rising from his seat. He already had a bottle of brandy in his hand.

'And what would you like, sir?'

'The same.'

James rested his elbows on the bar and asked:

'Did you go to the Taverne Royale? I thought so. I couldn't get there today . . .'

'Because of the 300,000 francs.'

James's face displayed neither surprise nor embarrassment.

'What would you have done in my place? Basso is a friend. We've drunk together hundreds of times. Cheers!'

'I'll leave you the bottle,' said the landlord. He was obviously used to James and was anxious to get back to his card game. James didn't seem to hear but continued:

'Basically he didn't have a chance. A woman like Mado. Talking of whom, have you seen her recently? She came by my office earlier to ask if I'd seen Marcel. Can you believe that? It's like that guy with his car. He's supposed to be a friend, but now he rings me to say that he's going to have to ask me to pay for the repairs and the charge for releasing his car from police custody. Your good health! What do you think of my wife? She's nice, isn't she?'

And James poured himself another glass of brandy.

7. The Second-Hand Dealer

There was something about James that Maigret found very interesting. As he drank, instead of becoming glassy-eyed, like most people, his gaze became more and more acute, until it acquired a sharpness that was almost penetrating.

He never removed his hand from his glass, except to refill it. His voice was slurred, faltering, lacking in conviction. He looked at no one in particular. He seemed to be melting into the background.

The card players at the back of the bar hardly spoke. The lights reflected dully off the zinc counter.

And James's voice was also dull when he sighed:

'It's weird. A man like you – strong, intelligent – and others too. Uniformed cops, judges, loads of people. How many are there involved in this? A hundred, maybe, if you include the clerks typing up the case notes, the telephonists passing on the orders . . . Let's call it a hundred people working day and night all because Feinstein got plugged by one tiny little bullet.'

He looked at Maigret, and the inspector was unable to tell whether he was being sincere or ironic.

'Cheers! It's all worth it, isn't it? And all this time poor old Basso is being hunted like an animal. Last week, he was rich. He had his business, his car, his wife and son. Now he can't stick his head out of his hole.'

James shrugged his shoulders. His voice slurred even more. He looked round the room with an expression of weariness or disgust.

'And what's it all about, eh? A woman like Mado with an appetite for men. Basso lets himself get snared – let's face it, you don't knock back opportunities like that when they come along. She's a good-looking girl. Spirited. You tell yourself it's just a bit of fun. You get together and spend an hour or two in a furnished apartment . . .'

James took a large swig then spat on the floor.

'Stupid, isn't it? One man ends up dead. A family is ruined. And the whole machinery of the law swings into action. Even the papers come along for the ride.'

The strangest thing was that there was no vehemence in his voice. He seemed to be talking aimlessly, gazing round the room at nothing in particular.

'And that's trumps,' the landlord said triumphantly from the back of the room.

'And Feinstein, who has spent his whole life chasing after money, trying to sort out his finances. Because that's what his life has been – one long nightmare of unpaid bills and invoices. To the point where he has to put the squeeze on his wife's lovers. And that's obviously worked well, now that he's dead . . .'

'Now that he's been killed,' Maigret corrected him dreamily.

'Do we really know which of the two actually killed the other?'

There was a heavy, morbid quality to James's words that fitted in with the growing gloom inside the bar.

'It's stupid! It's so obvious what happened. Feinstein needs money. He has been watching Basso since the previous evening, waiting for his chance. Even during the mock wedding, when he is dressed up as an old woman, he is still thinking about his debts! He watches Basso dancing with his wife. You see what I'm saying? So the next day he makes a move. Basso's been tapped for money before. He doesn't play ball. Feinstein won't give up that easily, pulls out his sob story: ruin, shame, he'd rather end it all now . . . the full works. I'd lay money on it being something like that. Just what you want on a fine Sunday afternoon by the river!

'Of course, it's all for effect. Feinstein is making it very clear that he is not as blind to his wife's peccadilloes as he likes to make out.

'Anyway, there they are behind the lean-to. Basso's thinking about his nice villa, his wife and kid across the river. He has to hush this whole thing up. He tries to stop him pulling the trigger, it's all getting out of hand, he makes a grab for the gun . . . then bang! That's it. One bullet from a tiny little revolver . . .'

James finally looked at Maigret.

'So I ask you. What the hell does any of this matter?'

He laughed. A laugh of contempt.

'And now we have hundreds of people scuttling around like ants who've just had their ant-hill set alight. The Bassos are being hunted like animals. And to cap it all, Mado still can't give up on her lover. Landlord!'

The landlord reluctantly put down his cards.

'What do I owe you?'

'But now Basso has 300,000 francs at his disposal.'

James merely shrugged his shoulders as if to reiterate his earlier question: 'What the hell does any of this matter?'

Then suddenly, he exclaimed:

'Wait! I remember how all this started. It was a Sunday. Some people were dancing in the garden of the villa. Basso was dancing with Madame Feinstein, and someone bumped into them, knocking them to the ground. They were lying there in each other's arms. Everyone laughed, including Feinstein.'

James picked up his change, but didn't seem to want to leave. Finally, he sighed:

'Another glass, landlord.'

He had downed six glasses, but he wasn't drunk. He must have had a bit of a sore head. He frowned and wiped his brow with his hand.

'Well, you've got to get back to the chase.'

He sounded like he felt sorry for Maigret.

'Three poor devils; a man, a woman and a child, all being hounded simply because the man slept with Mado.'

Was it his voice, his physical presence, the atmosphere of the bar? Whatever it was, he wove a fascinating spell, and Maigret was struggling to regain his objective view of the events that had taken place.

'Cheers, drink up. I'd better be getting back. I wouldn't put it past my wife to stick a bullet in me. It's stupid, stupid . . .'

He opened the door with a tired movement. Outside, in the badly lit street, he looked Maigret in the eyes and said:

'A strange occupation.'

'What? The police?'

'Just being a man . . . When I get home my wife will count the change in my pocket to see how much I've been drinking. Goodnight. See you in the Taverne Royale tomorrow?'

James went off, leaving Maigret with a sense of unease, which it took him a long time to shake off. It was as if all his thoughts had been unravelled and all his values had been turned on their head. Even the street looked distorted, the passers-by were a blur, and the long, thin trams were like brightly glowing worms.

It was like the ant-hill James had talked about. An ant-hill in a turmoil because one ant had been killed!

In his mind's eye, Maigret saw the haberdasher lying in the long grass behind the Two-Penny Bar. Then he saw all the police out manning the roadblocks. The ant-hill all stirred up!

'Drunken fool!' he murmured as he thought of James with a bitterness not altogether devoid of affection.

He made a fresh effort to look at the case objectively. He had forgotten what he had come to James's apartment to do – to find out where James had taken the 300,000 francs. But then he thought of the Basso family – the father, the mother and the child – skulking in their hideaway, jumping at the slightest noise from outside.

'That damn fellow gets me drinking every time we meet!'

He wasn't drunk, but he did feel out of sorts and went to bed in a bad mood, dreading the next day, when he would wake up with a thumping headache.

'You have to have a little bolt-hole to call your own,' James had said, talking of the Taverne Royale.

He didn't just have a bolt-hole, he inhabited a whole world of his own, totally self-contained, created in a haze of Pernod or brandy, in which he wandered around totally indifferent to the real world. It was a formless world, a teeming ant-hill of flitting shadows where nothing mattered, nothing had any purpose, where it was possible to wander aimlessly, effortlessly, feeling neither joy nor sadness, cocooned in a thick mist.

A world into which James, with his clownish manner and his apathetic way of talking, had sucked Maigret without seeming to do so.

So much so that the inspector found himself thinking about the Bassos – the father, the mother and the son – cowering in the cellar where they had sought refuge, listening anxiously to the footsteps coming and going over their heads.

When he got up he was even more conscious of the absence of his wife, from whom the postman delivered a postcard.

We are starting to make the apricot jam. When will you be coming to taste it?

He sat down heavily at his desk, causing the pile of letters in his in-tray to topple over. He called out, 'Come in!' to the clerk who was knocking at the door.

'What is it, Jean?'

'Sergeant Lucas has phoned asking for you to come to Rue des Blancs-Manteaux.'

'Which number?'

'He didn't say. He just said Rue des Blancs-Manteaux.'

Maigret checked that there wasn't anything in his mail that required urgent attention, then went on foot to the Jewish quarter, of which Rue des Blancs-Manteaux was the main shopping street, with a number of second-hand dealers huddled in the shadow of the large pawnshop.

It was 8.30 in the morning. It was quite quiet. At the corner of the street Maigret spotted Lucas, who was walking up and down with his hands in his pockets.

'Where's our man?' asked Maigret anxiously, for Lucas had been given the task of following Victor Gaillard after the latter's release the previous night.

With a movement of the head the officer pointed out the figure of a man standing in front of a shop window.

'What's he doing there?'

'I've no idea. Last night he wandered round Les Halles. He ended up dossing on a bench. At five o'clock this morning a policeman moved him on, and he made his way straight here. Ever since then he's been strolling round this house – occasionally wandering off then coming back again – pressing his nose against the window, all obviously for my benefit.'

Victor noticed Maigret and wandered off, his hands in his pockets, whistling ironically. He found a doorway and sat down in it, as if he had nothing better to do. The sign on the shop window read:

Hans Goldberg. Articles Bought and Sold. All Types of Bargains.

In the semi-darkness inside the shop sat a small man with a little goatee beard, who looked perturbed at the unusual activity outside his window.

'Wait here,' said Maigret.

He crossed the road and went inside the shop, which was stuffed with old clothes and a variety of other junk that gave off a musty odour.

'Are you looking for any item in particular?' the little Jew asked, not sounding terribly convinced that Maigret was a customer.

At the back of the shop there was a glass door leading into a room where a very fat woman was washing the face of a child of about two or three. The washbasin was placed on the kitchen table next to the cups and the butter dish.

'Police,' said Maigret.

'I suspected as much.'

'Do you know that person who's been hanging around in front of your shop all morning?'

'The tall thin chap with the cough? I've never seen him before. But his presence has been bothering me, and I asked my wife just earlier, but she didn't recognize him either. He's not an Israelite.'

'And do you recognize this man?'

Maigret held out a photo of Marcel Basso, which the man scrutinized intently.

'He's not an Israelite either!' he said.

'And this one?'

This time it was a picture of Feinstein.

'Yes!'

'You know him?'

'No, but he is one of us.'

'You've never seen him before?'

'Never. We don't go out much.'

His wife kept glancing at them through the door. She lifted another child out of a cradle, which began to howl when she started washing it.

The shopkeeper seemed quite sure of himself. He slowly rubbed his hands together as he awaited the inspector's next question and he looked round his shop with the satisfied expression of an honest tradesman with nothing to hide.

'How long have you owned this shop?'

'A little over five years. In that time I've established a reputation for fair dealing.'

'Who was here before you?' Maigret asked.

'You don't know? It was old Ulrich, the one who disappeared.'

The inspector gave a sigh of satisfaction. Finally he was on to something.

'Was Ulrich a second-hand dealer?'

'You should know better than I. Don't the police have records? I can't tell you anything definite. But I have heard people say that he didn't just buy and sell, he was also in the moneylending business.'

'He was a loan shark?'

'I don't know what his rate of interest was. He lived alone. He didn't have an assistant. He opened and closed up his shop himself. One day he disappeared, and the shop stayed closed for six months. I took it over. And I gave it a much better reputation altogether.'

'So you didn't know old Ulrich?'

'I didn't live in Paris at that time. I moved here from Alsace when I took over the shop.'

The baby was still crying in the other room; his brother had opened the door and was looking at Maigret and gravely sucking his finger.

'That's all I can tell you. Believe me, if I knew any more . . .'

'All right. That's fine.'

And Maigret went out after one last look around. He found Victor sitting in the doorway.

'Is this where you wanted to lead me?'

Victor feigned innocence:

'What do you mean?'

'I mean this business with old Ulrich?'

'Old Ulrich?'

'Stop messing about.'

'Don't know what you're talking about, honest.'

'Is he the one who took the plunge into the Canal Saint-Martin?'

'Dunno.'

Maigret shrugged his shoulders and walked away. As he passed Lucas, he said:

'Carry on keeping an eye on him, just in case.'

Half an hour later, he was searching through the old files. Finally he found what he was looking for. He summarized the details on a piece of paper:

Jacob Ephraïm Lévy, known as Ulrich, sixty-two years old, originally from Haute-Silésie, second-hand dealer in Rue des Blancs-Manteaux, suspected of usury.

Disappeared 20 March, though his neighbours did not alert the police until the 22nd.

No clues found at his house. Nothing was missing. A sum of 14,000 francs was discovered under his mattress.

As far as can be ascertained, he left home on the evening of the 19th. Nothing unusual in that.

No information on his private life. Inquiries in Paris and the provinces unsuccessful. The authorities in Haute-Silésie are informed, and one month later the sister of the missing man turns up in Paris to claim ownership of the property. She has to wait six months before he is officially declared missing presumed dead.

At midday Maigret, his head now aching, finally found some information in the heavy old registers of the police station at La Villette, the third he had visited that morning.

He transcribed the relevant passage:

On 1 July a body was pulled out of the Canal Saint-Martin, near the lock, by some bargees. The corpse was in an advanced state of decomposition.

The body was taken to the Forensic Institute, but it was not possible to make an identification.

Height: 1.55 m. Probable age: sixty to sixty-five.

Most of the clothing had been torn away on the canal bed and by boat propellers. Nothing found in the pockets.

Maigret heaved a sigh. He was finally emerging from the clouds of obfuscation that James seemed able to summon up at will to obscure the case.

Now he had something solid to work on. It was old Ulrich who was murdered six years ago and thrown into the Canal Saint-Martin.

Why? And by whom?

That was what he was going to find out. He filled his pipe and lit it slowly, with pleasure. He took his leave of his colleagues at La Villette and stepped out into the street, smiling, sure of himself, feeling solid on his sturdy legs.

8. James's Mistress

The chartered accountant came into Maigret's office rubbing his hands and looking pleased with himself.

'Got it!'

'What's that?'

'I've quickly gone through the haberdasher's books for the last seven years. It was easy. Feinstein didn't keep the books himself, but had a bank clerk come round two or three times a week to do them. Nothing out of the ordinary: just the usual tricks to minimize tax. But it's as plain as the nose on your face what was going on: the business would have been no worse than any other but for the lack of underlying capital. Suppliers paid on the 4th and 10th of every month, debts rescheduled two or three times, frequent sales to get some money in the tills at whatever cost. Finally, Ulrich!'

Maigret didn't react. He knew it would be better to let the voluble little man carry on talking, as he paced up and down the room.

'The classic story! Ulrich's name first appears in the books seven years ago. A loan of 2,000 francs to pay bills that had become due. Repaid a week later. The next billing date, a further loan of 5,000 francs. You see? He had found a way to get hold of cash when he needed it. He got into the habit. From that initial loan of 2,000, within six months he was borrowing 18,000. And this 18,000 cost him 25,000 to repay – old Ulrich liked to exact a price! I should say that Feinstein always honoured his debts, he always paid up on time. But he was paying off his debts by getting further into debt. For example, he repaid 15,000 francs on the 15th and borrowed another 17,000 on the 20th. He repaid this the following month, only to borrow 25,000 straight afterwards. By March, Feinstein owed Ulrich 32,000 francs.'

'Did he repay it?'

'I beg your pardon? From that date on Ulrich is never mentioned in the books again.'

And there was a very good reason for that: the old Jew from Rue des Blancs-Manteaux was dead, a death that left Feinstein the richer by 32,000 francs.

'Who took over from Ulrich?'

'No one, for a time. A year later, Feinstein was in trouble again and asked a small bank for credit, which he received. But the bank soon lost patience with him.'

'And Basso?'

'His name crops up in the later books – not under loans this time, but bills of exchange.'

'What was his situation like at the time of his death?'

'No better or worse than usual. He needed twenty grand to bale him out – at least until the next payment date! There are thousands of small traders in Paris in exactly the same situation – constantly chasing the exact sum they need to stop themselves tipping over the brink into bankruptcy.'

Maigret stood up and reached for his hat.

'Thank you, Monsieur Fleuret.'

'Do you want me to do a more in-depth analysis?'

'Not just yet.'

It was all going well. The inquiry was now running like clockwork. Paradoxically, Maigret was feeling down, as if he thought it was all falling into place rather too easily.

'Any news from Lucas?' he asked the clerk.

'He's just phoned. He said your man had gone to a Salvation Army hostel to ask for a bed. He's now sleeping.'

Of course Victor didn't have a single sou on him. Was he still hoping to receive 30,000 francs in return for the name of old Ulrich's murderer?

Maigret walked along the river. He hesitated in front of a post office, then went in and wrote a telegram:

Will probably arrive Thursday, stop. Love.

It was Monday. He hadn't been able to go and join his wife since the start of the holiday. He stuffed his pipe as he re-emerged on the street. He seemed to hesitate again, then he hailed a taxi and told the driver to take him to Boulevard des Batignolles.

He had handled hundreds of cases in his time, and he knew that they nearly always fell into two distinct phases. Firstly, coming into contact with a new environment, with people he had never even heard of the day before, with a little world which some event had shaken up.

He would enter this world as a stranger, an enemy; the people he encountered would be hostile, cunning or would give nothing away.

This, for Maigret, was the most exciting part. He would sniff around for clues, feel his way in the dark with nothing to go on. He would observe people's reactions – any one of them could be guilty, or complicit in the crime.

Suddenly he would get a lead, and then the second period would begin. The inquiry would be underway. The gears would start to turn. Each step in the inquiry would bring a fresh revelation, and nearly always the pace would quicken, so the final revelation, when it came, would feel sudden.

The inspector didn't work alone. The events worked for him, almost independently of him. He had to keep up, not be overtaken by them.

This was how it had been since the Ulrich discovery. Only this morning, Maigret had no clue as to the identity of the body in the Canal Saint-Martin.

Now he knew he was a second-hand dealer who doubled as a loan shark, to whom the haberdasher owed money.

Now he had to follow this thread. A quarter of an hour later, he was ringing the bell at the Feinsteins' apartment on the fifth floor of a building in Boulevard des Batignolles. A rather dim-looking maid with unkempt hair came to answer the door and seemed unsure whether she should let him in or not. But at that same moment Maigret spotted James's hat hanging in the hallway.

Was this the wheels of the case turning relentlessly onwards, or was it a spanner in the works?

*

'Is your mistress at home?'

The maid looked as if she was fresh up from the country, and he took advantage of her uncertainty to enter. He went to a door behind which he could hear voices, knocked and entered immediately.

He already knew the apartment. It was indistinguishable from most of the other lower-middle-class apartments in the area – a narrow sofa and rickety-looking armchairs with gilt feet. The first person he saw was James, who was standing in front of the window, staring out at the street.

Madame Feinstein was dressed to go out – all in black with a fetching little crêpe hat. She seemed extremely animated.

Despite this, she displayed no sign of annoyance when she saw Maigret, unlike James, who seemed put out, even embarrassed.

'Come in, inspector. You're not disturbing anything. I was just about to tell James how stupid he is.'

'Ah.'

It had all the appearance of a domestic tiff. James pleaded, with no great hope:

'Please, Mado . . .'

'No! Be quiet! I'm talking to the inspector.'

Resigned, James turned back to look at the street, where he could have seen little more than the heads of the passers-by.

'If you were an ordinary policeman, inspector, I wouldn't be talking to you like this. But as you were our guest at Morsang, and as you are clearly a man who is capable of understanding these things . . .'

And she was a woman who was capable of talking non-stop for hours, capable of calling the whole world as her witness, capable of reducing even the most talkative person to complete silence!

She wasn't especially beautiful. But she had a seductive quality, particularly in her mourning dress which, rather than giving her a sad appearance, made her look even more alluring. She was curvy, vivacious; she would have made an excellent mistress.

There couldn't be a greater contrast with the phlegmatic James, with his lugubrious face and his wandering gaze.

'Everyone knows I am Basso's mistress, don't they? I'm not ashamed of it. I've never made any secret of it. At Morsang, no one had any problem with it. If my husband had been a different sort of man . . .'

She barely paused for breath.

'If he'd been able to sort out his financial problems. Look at this dump. I have to live here. He was never around. Or when he was, in the evening after dinner, all he ever talked about was money problems, the business, his staff, stuff like that. But what I say is, if you can't give your wife the life she deserves, you can't complain if she goes off with someone else . . .

'Anyway, Marcel and I planned to get married one day. You didn't know? Naturally we didn't shout it from the rooftops. But for his son, he'd have started divorce proceedings already. I'd have done the same.

'You've seen his wife, haven't you? Not at all the sort of woman a man like Marcel needs.'

In the corner, James sighed. He was now staring at the carpet.

'Where do you think my duty lies? Marcel is in trouble, he's wanted by the police, he may have to go abroad. Don't you think that I should be there by his side? Tell me, just say what you think.'

'Hmm . . . well,' Maigret mumbled in a non-committal fashion.

'Exactly! You see, James? The inspector agrees with me. Never mind the gossip. I don't care what people think. But James won't tell me where I can find Marcel. He knows, I'm sure he does. He won't even deny it.'

Luckily Maigret had come across women like her before, otherwise he could have been suffocated by this tirade. He was not surprised by her complete lack of conscience.

It was less than two weeks since Feinstein had been killed, apparently by Basso.

And here was his wife, in their dreary apartment, with her husband's picture on the wall and his cigarette holder still in the ashtray, talking about her 'duty'.

James's face spoke volumes. Not just his face! His whole slumped posture seemed to be saying: 'Can you believe this woman?'

She turned towards him.

'You see, the inspector . . .'

'The inspector said no such thing.'

'I hate you! You're not a real man. You're afraid of everything. Suppose I tell him why you came here today . . .'

This took James so by surprise that his face went bright

red. He was blushing like a child, to the roots of his hair. He tried to speak, but the words didn't come out. He tried to regain his composure, but only managed to emit a strained laugh.

'Go on, you may as well tell him now.'

Maigret was watching the woman. She was a little thrown by what James had said.

'I didn't mean to . . .'

'No, you never mean to do anything! But you always end up doing it anyway!'

The room seemed smaller, more intimate. Mado shrugged her shoulders as if to say: 'Fine, I will. On your head be it.'

'Excuse me,' the inspector interjected, trying to keep a straight face as he spoke to James, 'I noticed you addressed her as *tu*. As I recall, in Morsang you were more formal . . .'

He could scarcely disguise his amusement, so great was the contrast between the James he knew and the sorry figure now standing in front of him. James had the look of a naughty schoolboy waiting outside the headmaster's study.

At his apartment, with his wife crocheting in the other corner, he had maintained a certain aloof demeanour.

Here, he seemed a stammering wreck.

'You must have worked it out by now. Yes, Mado and I were lovers too.'

'Luckily not for long,' she sneered.

He seemed disconcerted by this remark. He looked to Maigret for help.

'There you have it. It was a long time ago. My wife never knew about it.'

'And wouldn't she let you know about it if she did!'

'Knowing her as I do, I would never hear the last of it as long as I lived. So I came to ask Mado not to say anything if she was questioned.'

'And did she agree?'

'Only on the condition that I gave her Basso's current address. Can you believe that? He's with his wife and child. He's probably already left the country.'

He said that last bit less decisively. He was lying.

Maigret sat down in one of the armchairs, which gave a creak under his weight.

'Were you lovers for long?' he asked, like some friend of the family.

'Too long!' Madame Feinstein snapped.

'Not long . . . a few months,' James sighed.

'Did you meet in a furnished apartment like the one in the Avenue Niel?'

'No! James rented a place in Passy.'

'Were you already going to Morsang at the weekend?'

'Yes.'

'And Basso?'

'Yes. It's been the same gang for the last seven or eight years, with one or two exceptions.'

'Did Basso know you were lovers?'

'Yes. He wasn't in love with me then. He only became interested about a year ago.'

In spite of himself, Maigret felt jubilant. He looked round the little apartment, with its useless and rather hideous ornaments, and remembered James's rather more modern and pretentious studio, with its doll's house plywood partitions.

Then he thought of Morsang, the Vieux-Garçon, the canoes and sailing-boats, the rounds of drinks on the shady terrace, in a gentle, beautiful landscape.

For the last seven or eight years, every Sunday, the same group of people had been drinking aperitifs together, and playing bridge and dancing to records in the afternoon.

But in the beginning it was James who slipped off into the bushes with Mado. It was also he, no doubt, who first drew Feinstein's sarcastic gaze, he who had midweek rendezvous with her in Paris.

Everyone knew. Everyone turned a blind eye and was complicit in covering for Mado's affairs.

Among them her affair with Basso, who one day fell for her charms himself.

And now Maigret was enjoying this little scene in the apartment, what with James standing there looking pitiful and Mado forging on regardless.

It was to the latter that Maigret said:

'How long is it since you were James's mistress?'

'Let's see . . . five . . . no, six years, more or less.'

'And how did it end? Did he break it off or did you?'

James tried to speak, but she cut him off:

'It was mutual. We realized that we weren't right for each other. Despite his airs and graces, James is as petit bourgeois as they come. Perhaps even more so than my husband.'

'Did you remain good friends?'

'Of course, why not? It wasn't that we stopped liking each other . . .'

'One question for you, James. Did you lend any money to Feinstein around this time?'

'Me?'

But Mado answered his question:

'What are you driving at? Lend my husband money? Why?'

'No reason. Just idle curiosity. However, Basso did lend your husband money . . .'

'That's different. Basso is a wealthy man. My husband had financial problems. He was talking about taking me to America. Basso wanted to avoid any complications, so he lent him money . . .'

'That's all very well. But mightn't your husband have mentioned the possibility of going to America six years ago?'

'What are you insinuating?'

She was about to get on her high horse. Rather than face her blustering outrage, Maigret changed his tack:

'I'm sorry, I must have been thinking aloud. I assure you I didn't mean to insinuate anything. You and James were free agents. That's what a friend of your husband told me, a Monsieur Ulrich . . .'

Through half-closed eyes he observed both their reactions. Madame Feinstein looked surprised.

'A friend of my husband?'

'Or a business associate.'

'That's more likely. I've never heard that name mentioned. What did he say to you? . . .'

'Oh, nothing. We were discussing men and women in general.'

And James also looked surprised, but in the manner of a man who smells a rat and is trying to work out where this is all leading.

'This is all very well, but it doesn't get away from the fact that he knows where Marcel is and won't tell me,' said Madame Feinstein, rising from her chair. 'No matter, I'll find him myself. Anyway, he's bound to write to me to ask me to join him. He can't get by without me . . .'

James couldn't resist a sideways glance at Maigret, a look that was as mournful as it was ironic. It could be translated as: 'Do you think he's going to write to her? Do you think he wants a woman like her on his back all over again?'

She spoke to him:

'Is that your final word, James? Is that all the thanks I get, after everything I've done for you?'

'Have you done a lot for him?' Maigret asked.

'Why . . . he was my first lover! . . . Before he came along I'd never have dreamed of cheating on my husband. He was different then. He didn't drink. He looked after himself. He still had hair.'

And so the scales continued to oscillate between tragedy and complete farce. It was hard to hold on to the reality of the case: that Ulrich was dead, that someone had carried him to the Canal Saint-Martin, that six years later, behind the lean-to of the Two-Penny Bar, Feinstein had been shot dead and that Basso and his family were on the run from the police.

'Do you think he could have left the country, inspector?'

'I don't know . . .'

'If he needed your help you'd give it, wouldn't you? You've been his guest. You've seen what sort of man he is.'

'I have to get to the office! I'm already running late,' said James, searching each of the chairs for his hat.

'I'll come out with you,' Maigret added hastily. He certainly had no desire to be left alone with Madame Feinstein.

'Are you in a hurry?'

'I, er, have things to do, yes. But I'll be back.'

'Marcel will be grateful for your support. He knows how to show his appreciation.'

She was proud of her diplomatic skills. She could now envisage Maigret driving Basso to the border and being given a wad of banknotes for his pains.

When Maigret came to shake her hand, she held it for a long time, meaningfully. Indicating James, she murmured:

'We can't be too hard on him, what with his drinking and all.'

The two men didn't speak as they walked along Boulevard des Batignolles. James strode ahead, staring at the ground in front of him. Maigret puffed contentedly on his pipe and seemed to be enjoying the spectacle of the street.

It was only when they reached the corner of Boulevard Malesherbes that the inspector casually asked:

'Is it true that Feinstein never asked you for money?'

James shrugged his shoulders:

'He knew that I didn't have any.'

'Weren't you working at the bank in Place Vendôme?'

'No. At that time I was working as a translator for an American oil company in Boulevard Haussmann. I was earning less than a thousand francs a month.'

'Did you have a car?'

'I used the métro . . . as I still do, incidentally.'

'Did you have your apartment then?'

'No. We lived in a rented place on Rue de Turenne.'

He was tired. There was an expression of disgust on his face.

'Do you want a drink?'

And, without waiting for a reply, he went into the bar on the street corner and ordered two brandies and water.

'Personally, I couldn't give a damn. But I just don't want my wife to be bothered. She has enough troubles as it is.'

'Is she not well?'

Another shrug of the shoulders.

'You don't imagine she has much of a life, do you? Apart from Sundays at Morsang, where she can have a bit of fun.'

He threw a ten-franc note on to the counter, then changed the subject abruptly:

'Are you coming to the Taverne Royale tonight?'

'Maybe.'

As he came to shake Maigret's hand, he hesitated, looked away and murmured:

'What about Basso . . . have you discovered anything?'

'Classified information, I'm afraid,' said Maigret with a smile, full of bonhomie. 'You like him, don't you?'

But James was already on his way. He hopped on to a passing bus heading towards Place Vendôme.

Maigret stood there on the kerb for at least five minutes, quietly smoking his pipe.

9. Twenty-Two Francs of Ham

At Quai des Orfèvres they were looking for Maigret every-where, for he had been sent a telegram from the police station at La Ferté-Allais:

Basso family found. Await your instructions.

It had been a combination of scientific deduction and sheer luck.

The scientific part was the tests on the car that James abandoned at Montlhéry, tests which narrowed down the field of inquiry to a small sector centred on La Ferté-Allais.

Then the luck came into it. The police had searched all the inns and kept watch on the streets without success. They had even questioned a hundred or so people in the town, but had drawn a blank.

Then, on this same day, a policeman named Piquart came home for lunch as usual. His wife was feeding the baby, so she said to him:

'Could you nip down to the grocer's for some onions? I forgot to buy them earlier.'

A small-town grocer's shop on the market square. There were four or five shops in total. The policeman, who didn't much like these errands, stood by the door, looking unin-terested, while the grocer served an old woman known in

113

the town as old Mathilde. He overheard the grocer say to her:

'You're pushing the boat out. Twenty-two francs' worth of ham! Are you going to eat that all by yourself?'

Automatically, Piquart looked at the old woman, who was obviously very poor. And as the ham was being sliced, his brain began to whirr. Even at his house, where there were three of them, they never bought twenty-two francs' worth of ham at one go.

He followed the woman when she left the shop. She lived in a little house on the Bellancourt road, with hens pecking round in the small garden out the front. He let her go inside, then he knocked and asked to be let in in the name of the law.

Madame Basso was working at the kitchen stove, an apron tied round her waist. In the corner, sitting on a rush chair, Basso was reading the newspaper that the old woman had just brought him. The child was sitting on the floor, playing with a puppy.

The police had phoned Maigret's apartment in Boulevard Richard-Lenoir, then a few other places where he might have been found. They hadn't thought to try Basso's offices on the Quai d'Austerlitz.

For that is where he had gone after he had left James. He was in good humour. With his pipe in his mouth and his hands in his pockets he chatted and joked with the firm's employees, who, in the absence of instructions to the contrary, had carried on with business as usual. The barges were loaded and unloaded every day as normal.

The offices weren't especially up-to-date. But they weren't old-fashioned either. A quick look around was enough to get a sense of how the place was run.

The boss didn't have his own office, but had a desk in the corner, next to the window. The chief accountant sat opposite him, and his secretary was at a desk nearby.

Obviously, this wasn't a hierarchical place. People seemed free to chat, and many of them worked with a pipe or a cigarette in their mouth.

'An address book?' the accountant responded to the inspector's request. 'Yes, of course we have one, but it only contains the addresses of our customers in alphabetical order. If you wish to see it . . .'

Maigret had a quick look at the letter U, but, as he had expected, the name of Ulrich wasn't there.

'Are you sure Monsieur Basso doesn't have a private address book? . . . Hold on, who was working here when his son was born?'

'I was,' the secretary replied, a little reluctantly, for she was a thirty-five-year-old who wanted to pass herself off as twenty-five.

'Good. Monsieur Basso must have sent out announcements.'

'He did. I took care of that.'

'Then he must have given you a list of his friends' names.'

'Yes, that's right, he gave me a little notebook! I filed it away with his personal items.'

'Where is the file?'

She hesitated, looked to her colleagues for guidance.

The chief accountant shrugged as if to say: 'I don't see that we have any choice.'

'It's up at the house,' she said. 'Would you care to follow me?'

They walked across the yard. On the ground floor of the house, there was a simply furnished study that looked as if it was never used. In fact, it was known as the library.

The library of a family for whom reading came well down the list of distractions. A family library, used as the dumping-ground for a whole host of disparate objects.

For example, on the lower shelves were the prizes Basso had won at school. Then some bound volumes of *Magazine des Familles* dating back fifty years.

Some books for young girls that Madame Basso must have brought with her when she got married. Then a number of serious novels bought on the strength of favourable newspaper reviews.

Finally some brand-new picture books belonging to the child and some toys stored on the remaining empty shelves.

The secretary opened the drawers of the desk, and Maigret noticed a fat yellow envelope that was sealed.

'What's that?'

'Monsieur's letters to madame when they were engaged.'

'Have you found the notebook?'

She discovered it at the bottom of a drawer that contained a dozen or so old pipes. It looked at least fifteen years old. It was in Basso's hand, though his writing had changed over time, and the ink had faded.

It was like the lines of seaweed on a beach, showing

which tide had washed them up by how dried out they were.

The addresses were fifteen years old, addresses of friends now no doubt forgotten. A few had been crossed out, perhaps because of some falling out, or because the person in question had died.

There were a number of addresses of women, such as:

Lola, Bar des Églantiers, 18, Rue Montaigne.

But Lola had been erased from Basso's life by a blue pencil.

'Have you found what you're looking for?' the secretary asked.

He had indeed! A name the coal merchant was ashamed of, for he hadn't written it out in full:

Ul. 13 bis, Rue des Blancs-Manteaux.

The ink and the handwriting suggested this was an old entry. It was one of those addresses with a blue line through it, though it was still legible underneath.

'Can you tell me approximately when these words were written?'

The secretary bent over to take a closer look.

'It was when Monsieur Basso was a young man, and his father was still alive.'

'How can you tell?'

'Because it is written in the same ink as the woman's

address on the other page. He once told me he had a fling with her in his younger days.'

Maigret closed the notebook and slipped it into his pocket, despite the disapproving look he received from the secretary.

'Do you think he will come back?' she asked, after a slight hesitation.

The inspector gave a non-committal shrug.

When he got back to the Quai des Orfèvres, Jean, the office clerk, ran up to meet him.

'We've been looking for you for the last two hours. They've found the Bassos.'

'Ah!'

He gave a mighty sigh, which almost sounded like a sigh of regret.

'Has Lucas phoned?'

'He calls in every three or four hours. Your man is still at the Salvation Army hostel. They wanted to turf him out after they had fed him, but he offered to sweep up around the place.'

'Is Janvier here?'

'I believe he's just got back.'

Maigret went to Janvier's office.

'I've got just the sort of awkward job you like, my friend. I want you to track down a certain Lola, who gave her postal address as the Bar des Églantiers, Rue Montaigne, about ten to fifteen years ago.'

'And since then?'

'Who knows? She could have died in hospital. She could have married an English lord . . . Get cracking.'

On the train journey to La Ferté-Allais he examined the address book, smiling every now and again at certain entries that seemed so evocative of how it felt to be young, free and single.

A police lieutenant was waiting for him at the station. He drove the inspector to old Mathilde's house, where they found Piquart gravely standing guard in the small front garden.

'We've made sure that there is no way of escape at the back,' the lieutenant explained. 'It's just so small inside that my officer has to stand out the front. Do you want me to come in with you?'

'Perhaps it would be better if you stayed out here.'

Maigret knocked at the door, which opened immediately. It was late. It was still light outside, but the window was so narrow that inside the house he could see little more than moving shadows.

Basso was straddling a chair in the pose of a man who had been waiting for a long time. He got to his feet. His wife and child must have been in the adjoining room.

'Could we have some light?' Maigret asked the old woman.

'I'll have to see if there's any oil in the lamp,' she replied tartly.

It turned out that there was. The glass was replaced with a clink, the wick began first to smoke, then to burn with a yellow flame that gradually filled the corners of the room with light. It was quite hot inside the house. A smell of the countryside, of poverty.

'Do sit down,' Maigret told Basso. 'If you wouldn't mind leaving us alone, madame.'

'What about my soup?'

'Off you go. I'll keep an eye on it.'

She went away grumbling to herself and shut the door behind her. In the adjoining room she could be heard speaking in a low voice.

'Are there just the two rooms?' the inspector asked.

'Yes. The room at the back is the bedroom.'

'Is that where the three of you have been sleeping?'

'The two women and my son. I've been sleeping in here on a straw bale.'

There were bits of straw still lodged in the cracks between the uneven floor tiles. Basso was calm, but it was the sort of calm that follows on from several days of fever. It was as if he were somehow relieved to be arrested. Indeed, the first thing he said was:

'I was going to turn myself in.'

He was probably expecting Maigret to be surprised by this, but the latter showed no reaction. The inspector didn't even say a word. He merely looked at Basso from head to toe.

'Isn't that one of James's suits?'

It was a grey suit, too tight. Basso had broad shoulders and was as sturdily built as Maigret. Nothing can diminish a man in the prime of his life as much as a set of ill-fitting clothes.

'Obviously you know already . . .'

'I know lots of things besides . . . But do you think we should take this soup off the stove?'

The pan was belching out steam, and the lid was rattling under the pressure. Maigret removed the pan from the heat, and his face was momentarily lit up by the red flames.

'You knew old Mathilde before?'

'I wanted to talk to you about her. I don't want her to get into trouble because of me. She used to be my parents' servant. She's known me since I was a boy. When I came here looking for a place to hide, she couldn't turn me away.'

'Of course not. It's just a shame she made the mistake of buying twenty-two francs' worth of ham at one go.'

Basso had lost a lot of weight. He hadn't shaved for four or five days. In all, he looked a bit of a mess.

'I also trust that my wife has nothing to answer for . . .' he sighed.

He stood up, looking stiff and awkward, like someone trying to find the right way to broach a weighty topic.

'I was wrong to run away, to stay in hiding for so long. But maybe that shows that I am not a real criminal. Do you understand? I lost my head. I saw my life in ruins because of this stupid affair. I thought I would go abroad, have my wife and child come out to join me and try to start a new life.'

'And you got James to bring your wife here, to withdraw 300,000 francs from the bank and to bring you a change of clothes.'

'Yes.'

'Only, you realized that you were being pursued.'

'Old Mathilde told me there were policemen at every crossroads.'

There was still some noise coming from next door. The child must have been moving about. Madame Basso was probably listening at the door because every now and again they heard her say 'Shush!' to the child.

'Today I came to the only possible conclusion: I had to give myself up. But fate decreed otherwise, and the policeman turned up . . .'

'Did you kill Feinstein?'

Basso looked Maigret straight in the eye.

'I did,' he said quietly. 'It would be mad to deny it, wouldn't it? But I swear on my son's life that I will tell you the whole truth.'

'Just a moment.'

Maigret now got to his feet. And they stood there, both more or less the same build, under the low ceiling, in a room that was too small for them.

'Did you love Mado?'

Basso's lip curled in bitterness.

'You're a man, you should understand. I've known her for six or seven years, maybe more. I'd never given her a second glance before. Then one day, about a year ago, I don't know what happened. It was a party, like the one you came to. We were drinking, dancing . . . I ended up kissing her . . . then we slipped off to the bottom of the garden.'

'And then?'

He gave a tired shrug.

'She took it all seriously. She swore she'd always been in love with me, that she couldn't live without me. I'm no saint. I admit that I started it. But I didn't want to get that involved, I didn't want to jeopardize my marriage.'

'So you've been seeing Madame Feinstein in Paris two or three times a week for the last year . . .'

'And she's been phoning me every day! I've pleaded with her to be more careful, but it's no use. She's always come up with some ridiculous excuse. I was sure we'd be discovered any day. You can't imagine what that was like . . . If only she wasn't so sincere. But no! I think she really did love me.'

'And Feinstein?'

Basso looked up suddenly.

'Oh yes,' he groaned. 'That's why I couldn't bear the thought of having to defend myself in court. There are limits in these compromising situations. There's only so much the public will swallow. Can you see me, Mado's lover, standing up in court, accusing her husband of . . .'

'. . . of blackmailing you.'

'I don't have any proof. He was and he wasn't. He never explicitly said that he knew anything was going on. He never threatened me directly. You know what he was like – an inoffensive little man, wouldn't hurt a fly. A weedy-looking chap, always smartly dressed, always polite – too polite. That hangdog smile of his . . . The first time he came to me with a problem concerning a protested bill and begged me to lend him some money. He offered me all sorts of assurances. I did as he asked. I would have done anyway, even without Mado.

'However, this turned into something of a routine. I realized it was quite calculated. I tried to refuse. That's when the blackmail began. He took me into his confidence. He said his wife was his only consolation. It was because of her that he had taken on expenses he couldn't afford and had got himself into this bind, etcetera. And he'd rather kill himself than refuse her anything she wanted. And if he did, what would become of her?

'Can you believe it? He always managed to show up just after I had left Mado. I was afraid he would be able to smell her perfume on my clothes. One time he picked a woman's hair – one of hers – off the collar of my jacket.

'He was never threatening. More whining, which is worse! At least you can defend yourself against threats. But what do you do with a man who cries? Yes, I've actually had him in my office in tears.

'And the things he came out with: "You're young, you're strong, you're good-looking, you're rich . . . A man like you has no trouble finding someone to love him . . . But what about me? . . ." It made me sick. And yet I could never be absolutely certain that he knew.

'That Sunday, he had already spoken to me before we played bridge and had asked me to lend him 15,000 francs. It was too much. I wouldn't play ball. I'd had enough. So I just said no, straight out. And I said I wouldn't see him again if he continued to harass me in this way.

'So that's how it all blew up, the whole stupid, sordid little mess. If you recall, he arranged it so that we sailed across the river at the same time. He dragged me behind the bar. Then, suddenly, he pulled a small revolver from his pocket and pointed it at his own head, saying, "This is what you've brought me to . . . I ask just one thing of you. Take care of Mado when I'm gone . . ."'

Basso ran his hand across his brow, as if trying to wipe away this wretched memory.

'It was just bad luck. I felt light-headed that day. Perhaps it was the sun. I went up to him to try to grab the gun.

'"No, no!" he cried. "You're too late. It's you who have brought me to this!"'

'Naturally, he had no intention of pulling the trigger,' Maigret muttered.

'I know. That's why the whole thing is so tragic. I lost my head. I should have left well alone and nothing would have come of it. He'd have burst into tears again, or extricated himself some other way. But no! I was a naive fool. Like I was with Mado. Like I've always been.

'I tried to grab the revolver off him. He retreated, but I went after him. I grabbed him by the wrist. Then it happened. The gun went off. Feinstein fell, without a word, without a sound. Dropped like a stone . . .

'Not that a jury will believe me. Nor will the judges be any less hard on me. I'll be the man who killed his mistress's husband and then accused the dead man of blackmail.'

He was becoming quite animated.

'I wanted to run away. And I did. I also wanted to tell my wife everything, ask her whether, in spite of everything, she still wanted me as her husband. I wandered round Paris, hoping to find James. He's a friend, probably my only real friend in the Morsang crowd.

'You know the rest. My wife knows too. I'd rather we'd got away abroad and avoided this trial, which will be very painful for all concerned. I have the 300,000 francs here.

What with that and my head for business, I'd have been able to start afresh somewhere – in Italy, for example, or Egypt.

'But . . . do you believe what I've just told you?'

He faltered all of a sudden. But the doubt was merely momentary, so caught up was he in what he was saying.

'I believe you didn't mean to kill Feinstein,' Maigret replied, slowly, articulating each word carefully.

'You see! . . .'

'Wait a minute. What I want to know is whether or not Feinstein had a stronger card to play than his wife's infidelity. In short . . .'

He paused while he took the little address book from his pocket and opened it at the letter U.

'In short, I would like to know who killed a certain Monsieur Ulrich, a second-hand dealer of Rue des Blancs-Manteaux, six years ago, and subsequently threw his body into the Canal Saint-Martin.'

He almost didn't finish his sentence, so violent was the change in Basso's demeanour. So violent, in fact, that he almost lost his balance and, in seeking to grab hold of something, placed his hand on the stove and then withdrew it with an oath.

'My God!'

He stared at Maigret, wide-eyed with horror. He recoiled until he bumped into his chair, and he collapsed into it, looking completely drained of strength.

'My God!'

The door burst open and Madame Basso rushed into the room screaming:

'Marcel! . . . Marcel! . . . It can't be true! . . . Tell me it's not true!'

He looked at her uncomprehendingly, perhaps not even seeing her. Suddenly he choked; he put his head in his hands and started sobbing.

'Papa! . . . Papa!' the child yelped, dashing in to add to the confusion.

Basso didn't hear anything. He pushed away his wife and son. He was totally crushed, unable to control his tears. He sat bent over in his chair, his shoulders heaving in time with his racking sobs.

The child was crying too. Madame Basso bit her lip, sending Maigret a look of pure hatred.

And old Mathilde, who hadn't dared to come in, but who had witnessed everything through the open door, also cried, the way old women cry: short, regular sobs, wiping her eyes with the corner of her checked apron.

Yet despite her tears and sniffles, she managed to put her soup pan back on the stove, stoking the flames to life with a poker.

10. *Inspector Maigret's Absence*

Scenes like this don't last long. The nervous system can only take so much. Once the crisis has reached its pitch, a sudden flat calm sets in, a calm as numb as the preceding fever was manic.

We are then supposed to feel shame, shame for the frenzy, the tears, for the things we said, as if such emotion were somehow not human.

Maigret waited, feeling awkward, looking out of the little window at the policeman's cap silhouetted against the darkening sky. He was conscious nonetheless of what was going on behind him – Madame Basso going up to her husband, grabbing him by the shoulders and pleading in her hoarse voice:

'Just tell me it isn't true!'

Basso sniffed, got to his feet, pushed his wife away and looked around him with the glassy-eyed gaze of a drunk. The door of the stove was open. The old woman was feeding it with coal. It threw a large circle of red light on to the ceiling, causing the beams to stand out.

The boy looked at his father and, in copycat fashion, stopped crying also.

'I'm done now . . . I'm sorry for all that,' said Basso, now standing in the centre of the room.

He seemed poleaxed. His voice dwindled away. He didn't have an ounce of strength left in him.

'Do you confess?'

'No, I've got nothing to confess. Listen . . .'

He looked at his family with a wounded expression, his brow furrowed deeply.

'I didn't kill Ulrich. The reason I broke down just now was because I . . . I realized that . . .'

He was so drained he could hardly find the words.

'That you couldn't prove your innocence?'

He nodded. Then he said:

'I didn't kill him.'

'You said those same words right after Feinstein was killed. Yet you have just confessed to that.'

'That's different . . .'

'Did you know Ulrich?'

A bitter smile.

'Look at the date on the first page of the notebook. Twelve years ago. It was about ten years ago that I saw Ulrich for the last time.'

He had recovered some of his composure, but his voice still displayed the same despair.

'My father was still alive. Talk to anyone who knew him and you'll hear what a hard man he was. Strict on himself and on others. I was given a smaller allowance than even the poorest of my friends. So someone took me to see old Ulrich in Rue des Blancs-Manteaux, who had some experience of these matters.'

'And you didn't know he was dead?'

Basso said nothing. Maigret repeated his question without drawing breath:

'You didn't know he had been killed, driven in a car to the Canal Saint-Martin and thrown into the lock?'

Basso didn't reply. His shoulders became even more hunched. He looked at his wife, his son and the old woman, who were laying the table despite their tears, simply because it was dinnertime.

'What are you going to do?'

'I'm arresting you. Madame Basso and your son can stay here, or go home.'

Maigret opened the front door and said to the policeman:

'Bring a car round.'

A crowd of onlookers had gathered in the road, but like the prudent peasants they were, they kept their distance. When Maigret turned round, Madame Basso was in her husband's arms. He was mechanically patting her back, while staring into space.

'Promise me you'll take care of yourself,' she murmured. 'And don't do anything stupid.'

'Yes.'

'Swear!'

'Yes.'

'Think of your son, Marcel!'

'Yes,' he repeated with a trace of annoyance in his voice, as he disentangled himself from her embrace.

Was he afraid of being overcome by emotion again? He waited impatiently for the car he had heard Maigret order.

He didn't want to say anything, listen to anything, look at anything. His fingers trembled constantly.

'You didn't kill this man, did you? Listen to me, Marcel. You have to listen to me. They won't condemn you for . . . for the other business. You didn't mean to do it. And we can prove that this man was a wicked person. I'll find a good lawyer straight away. The best . . .'

She was speaking vehemently. She wanted to make sure she was heard.

'Everyone knows you're a good man. We can probably get you out on bail. Just don't let it get on top of you. Just remember . . . that other crime wasn't anything to do with you.'

She looked at Maigret defiantly.

'I'll see a lawyer tomorrow. I'll get my father up from Nancy, to give me some advice. Come on, we can get through this . . .'

She didn't realize that she was hurting him, by threatening to remove the last shred of composure he possessed. He was trying to ignore her, straining to hear the sounds from outside. He was aching for the car to arrive.

'I'll come and see you. I'll bring the boy.'

Finally there was the sound of the car pulling up. Maigret brought the scene to a conclusion.

'Let's go.'

'You promised, Marcel!'

She couldn't let him go. She pushed their son towards him, to melt his heart further. Basso was already walking down the three steps outside the house.

Then she grabbed Maigret's arm so firmly she pinched it.

'Watch him!' she panted. 'Watch him carefully. Make sure he doesn't kill himself. I know what sort of man he is.'

She noticed the group of onlookers but gave them a bold, unrepentant look.

'Wait! Your scarf!'

She ran back inside the house to fetch it, and handed it through the window of the car as it was pulling away.

In the car, Basso, now he was in the company of men, seemed to relax slightly. He sat there with Maigret for a good ten minutes without either of them saying a word. It was only when they reached the main road that Maigret spoke, his words seeming to bear no relation to the drama that had just taken place.

'You have an admirable wife.'

'Yes, she understood. Perhaps it is because she is a mother. I don't know that I'd be able to explain why I got involved with . . . with that woman.'

There was a pause. Then he continued in a confidential tone:

'At the time, you don't think. It's a game, and you don't quite have the courage to break it off. You're afraid there'll be a scene, you're scared of the recriminations. And so this is where you end up.'

There was nothing to see out of the window except the trees flashing past, illuminated by the car's headlights. Maigret filled his pipe and offered Basso his tobacco pouch.

'No, thank you. I only smoke cigarettes.'

It helped somehow to have some ordinary conversation.

'I noticed you had a dozen or so pipes in your drawer at home.'

'Yes. At one time I used to be a keen pipe-smoker. My wife asked me to stop . . .'

His voice faltered. Maigret noticed his eyes filling with tears. He hastily changed the subject:

'Your secretary seems very loyal too.'

'She's a good girl. She looks after me really well. She must be devastated.'

'I'd say she was fairly optimistic. She was asking when you would be coming back. All in all, you seem to be well liked.'

They fell silent again. They were now passing through Juvisy. At Orly, they saw the airfield searchlights raking the sky.

'Was it you who gave Feinstein Ulrich's address?'

But Basso refused to answer.

'Feinstein had lots of dealings with him. His name crops up in the accounts, along with the sums involved. At the time that Ulrich was murdered, Feinstein owed him at least 30,000 francs.'

No, Basso wouldn't reply. He sat there in obstinate silence.

'What is your father-in-law's profession?'

'He is a teacher in a school in Nancy. My wife trained as a teacher also.'

And so the conversation proceeded, drifting close to the trauma of recent events, then receding to the safety of small talk. At times Basso spoke quite normally, as if he had forgotten his situation. Then came tense silences, pregnant with unspoken thoughts.

'Your wife is right. In the Feinstein case you have a good chance of being acquitted. At worst you may get a year in prison. As for the Ulrich case, however . . .'

Then, abruptly, he went on:

'I'm going to put you in the cell at police headquarters tonight. Tomorrow we can get you transferred to a remand prison.'

Maigret tapped out his pipe and wound down the glass screen to speak to the driver:

'Quai des Orfèvres! Go straight into the courtyard.'

Then without further ado, the inspector led Basso to the cell where Victor had been locked up.

'Goodnight,' said Maigret, after checking that he had everything he needed in the cell. 'I'll see you tomorrow. Have a think. Are you sure that you have nothing to say to me?'

Basso was perhaps too full of emotion to speak. He merely shook his head.

Confirm will arrive Thursday, stop. Will stay a few days, stop. Love.

It was Wednesday morning when Maigret wrote the telegram to his wife. He was in his office at the Quai des Orfèvres and he gave it to Jean to take to the post office.

A short while later, the examining magistrate in charge of the Feinstein case phoned him. Maigret told him:

'I hope to be able to give you my completed case report

by this evening . . . Yes, of course, the guilty party too . . . No, no, not at all. Just a standard, open-and-shut case . . . Yes! Talk to you this evening. Goodbye.'

He got up and went into the operations room, where he found Lucas typing up a report.

'How's our vagrant?'

'I've handed over to Dubois. Nothing much to report. You know Victor started doing some work at the Salvation Army hostel. He seemed to get well into it. He'd told them about his lung, of course, so they were especially keen to help him out. I think they'd started to regard him as a potential recruit. Who knows, we could have been seeing him in his uniform in a month or so.'

'What happened?'

'It's quite amusing. Yesterday evening a Salvation Army lieutenant asked him to do something or other. He refused and started kicking up a fuss about how he was being made to work like a dog despite all his afflictions. They asked him to leave, and it ended up in fisticuffs. He had to be thrown out by force. He spent the night kipping under the Pont Marie. Now he's hanging about down by the river. Dubois will be ringing in soon to bring you up to date.'

'I won't be here, so tell him to bring him in and lock him in the cell with the other person who's in there.'

'OK.'

Maigret went home and spent the rest of the morning packing. He had lunch in a brasserie near Place de la République, checked the railway timetable and found that there was a handy train to Alsace at 10.40 in the evening.

These leisurely activities kept him occupied until four

o'clock in the afternoon, when he set off for the Taverne Royale. He had barely taken his place on the terrace when James turned up. They shook hands, and James looked round for a waiter as he asked Maigret:

'Pernod?'

'Why not?'

'Waiter, two Pernods!'

James crossed his legs, sighed and looked straight ahead like a man with nothing to say and nothing on his mind. It had clouded over. Unexpected gusts of wind swept the street, raising plumes of dust.

'There's going to be a storm,' James sighed. Then abruptly: 'Is it true what I read in the papers? You've arrested Basso?'

'Yes. Yesterday afternoon.'

'Cheers. It's stupid.'

'What's stupid?'

'What he did. A solid, respectable man like him losing his head like that. He'd have been better advised to turn himself in at the start and defend himself. What did he really have to lose?'

Maigret had already heard Madame Basso give the same speech and he smiled to himself.

'Your good health. Maybe you're right, maybe you're wrong.'

'What do you mean? It wasn't premeditated murder, was it? You can hardly even call it a crime.'

'Quite. If Basso had only the death of Feinstein to answer for, then we could say he simply lost his head in a moment of weakness.'

Then, with a suddenness that made James jump, he called out:

'Waiter! What do I owe you?'

'Six-fifty.'

'You're leaving?'

'I have to go and see Basso.'

'Ah.'

'Would you like to see him? You can come too.'

In the taxi they made small talk.

'How's Madame Basso bearing up?'

'She's a very brave woman. And very cultured too. I wouldn't have thought that, seeing her that Sunday at Morsang in her sailing clothes.'

And Maigret asked him:

'How is your wife?'

'Fine, as usual.'

'Not too upset by recent events?'

'Why would she be? She's not the worrying sort. She takes care of the housework, she sews, she does her embroidery, she goes shopping, likes looking for bargains.'

'We're here. This way.'

Maigret steered his companion across the courtyard. He asked the officer guarding the cell:

'Are they here?'

'Yes.'

'Everything peaceful?'

'Apart from the new one Dubois brought in this morning. Says he's going to appeal to the League of Human Rights.'

Maigret barely smiled. He opened the door of the cell and let James go in first.

There was only one bunk, and Victor was occupying it. He had taken off his jacket and sandals.

Basso was walking up and down with his hands behind his back when they came in. He looked at them both, questioningly, then fixed his eyes on Maigret.

Victor stood up grumpily, then sat down again, muttering inaudibly to himself.

'I bumped into James and I thought you'd like to see him.'

'Hello, James,' said Basso, shaking his hand.

But there was something missing. It was difficult to pinpoint. There was a certain reserve, a certain chill in the atmosphere. Maigret realized he would have to force the pace.

'Gentlemen,' he began, 'please take a seat, for we may be some time. You, make some room on the bunk. And please try to refrain from coughing for the next quarter of an hour. It cuts no ice in here.'

Victor merely sneered, like a man who was happy to bide his time.

'Take a seat, James. You too, Monsieur Basso. Excellent. Now, if you're sitting comfortably, I would like to take a few moments to recap the story so far.

'Some time ago, a man named Lenoir was sentenced to death. Before his execution he made an accusation against a certain individual whom he refused to name. It concerned an old case whose perpetrator no doubt felt was now safely gathering dust. Briefly, around six years ago a car drove away from an address in Paris and headed towards the Canal Saint-Martin. There, the driver lifted a body from the car and dropped it into the water.

'No one would have known a thing about it but for the fact that the whole scene was witnessed by two young villains by the name of Lenoir and Victor Gaillard. It didn't cross their minds to inform the police. They preferred to profit from their discovery, and so they traced the murderer and extorted various sums of money from him over a period of time.

'However, being still novices, they failed to take adequate precautions. One fine day they discovered that their cash cow had upped and left.

'And there we have it. The victim was called Ulrich. He was a Jewish second-hand dealer who lived on his own and consequently was missed by no one.'

Maigret slowly lit his pipe without looking at his audience. Nor did he look at them when he started talking again, but rather stared at his feet the whole time.

'Six years later, Lenoir came across the murderer again quite by chance, but he was unable to resume his lucrative business because he was caught for a crime of his own and sentenced to death.

'Now, listen carefully. Before he died, as I mentioned, he said a few things that narrowed down the field to a very select group of people. He also wrote to his former colleague to inform him of the discovery, and he hot-footed it to the Two-Penny Bar.

'And so we come, as it were, to the second act. Don't

interrupt, James! Same goes for you, Victor. We come to the Sunday when Feinstein was killed. Ulrich's murderer was at the Two-Penny Bar that day. It could have been you, Basso, or me, or you, James, or Feinstein, or someone else. Only one person can tell us for certain, and that's Victor Gaillard, here present.'

Victor opened his mouth to speak, and Maigret literally shouted:

'Silence!'

Then, in a quieter tone, he continued:

'Now the said Victor Gaillard, who is a cunning little lowlife, doesn't want to give up the information for free. He wants 30,000 francs in return for the name. Let's say he'll settle for twenty-five. Silence, I say! Let me finish! Now the police are not in the habit of doling out such large sums of money, so all they can do for Gaillard is to pursue him on a charge of blackmail.

'Let us consider the various suspects. As I said earlier, all the people who were at the Two-Penny Bar on the Sunday in question could be under suspicion. Some more than others, however. For example, it is a fact that Basso once knew Monsieur Ulrich. It is also a fact not only that Feinstein knew him, but that the moneylender's death meant he didn't have to repay the considerable sum of money he owed him.

'Feinstein is dead. From what we have gathered, it is clear he was not a nice person to know. If he killed Ulrich, then the case is closed and no further action is required. Victor Gaillard could confirm this, but I am not in a position to accept his blackmail . . . Silence! You will have a chance to speak when you are questioned.'

Victor was getting quite worked up and was trying to interrupt the inspector at every opportunity. Maigret still did not look at any of them. He had been speaking in a monotonous tone, as if reciting a lesson. Suddenly he went to the door, murmuring:

'I'll be back in a minute. I have an important phone call to make.'

The door opened, then closed behind him. Then the sound of his steps faded away up the stairs.

11. Ulrich's Murderer

Maigret was talking to the examining magistrate on the phone.

'Hello! Yes! Just give me another ten minutes . . . His name? I don't know yet . . . Yes, of course I'm serious. Do I ever joke about these things?'

He put down the receiver and started walking up and down his office. He went over to Jean.

'By the way, I'll be away for a few days. Here is the address for forwarding my mail.'

He kept looking at his watch, then finally decided to go back down to the cell where he had left the three men.

When he came in, the first thing he saw was Victor's hate-filled face. He was no longer sitting on the bed, but was pacing angrily round the cell. Basso was sitting on the edge of the bunk with his head in his hands.

As for James, he was leaning against the wall with his arms folded, and he looked at Maigret with a strange smile.

'I'm sorry for keeping you waiting. I . . .'

'It's over,' said James. 'You didn't need to pull that stunt with the phone call.'

And his smile grew broader the more Maigret looked discomfited.

'Victor Gaillard will not earn his 30,000 francs, either

by talking or by keeping his mouth shut. I killed Ulrich.'

The inspector opened the door and called to an officer who was passing:

'Lock this man up somewhere until I'm ready for him.'

He indicated Victor, who was still shouting:

'Don't forget it was me who led you to Ulrich! Without me, you'd be nowhere. And that's worth . . .'

Maigret now found this obstinate persistence in trying to extract a profit from the case not so much contemptible as pathetic.

'Five thousand! . . .' he shouted as he was hauled up the stairs.

Now there were three of them in the cell. Basso was the most downcast of the three. He remained sitting a good while before standing up and facing Maigret.

'I swear I was willing to pay the 30,000 francs, inspector. What is that to me? But James wouldn't let me.'

Maigret looked from one to the other with an astonishment coloured by a growing sympathy.

'You knew about this, Basso?'

'I've known for a long time,' he murmured.

James filled in the details:

'He was the one who gave me the money those two tykes were extorting from me. So I told him the whole story.'

'This is crazy. For just 30,000 francs we could have . . .'

'No! No,' James sighed. 'You don't understand. Nor does the inspector.'

He looked round as if he was searching for something. 'Anyone got a cigarette?'

Basso gave him his cigarette case.

'I suppose a Pernod's out of the question? No matter. I'll have to get used to it. All the same, it would have made this easier.'

He licked his lips like a drinker suffering withdrawal.

'Actually, there's not much to say. I was married. Nice peaceful little marriage, a quiet life. I met Mado. And stupidly I thought I'd hit the jackpot. Just like in the novels. *My life for a kiss . . . Live life like there's no tomorrow . . . Leave the world behind . . .*'

The phlegmatic way he said all this made his confession sound dispassionate, not quite human, as if he was performing in a burlesque.

'When you're at that age it's all very exciting. Secret trysts in rented rooms, glasses of port and petits fours. But that all costs money. I was earning a thousand francs a month. And therein lay the roots of the whole sorry, sordid mess. I couldn't talk to Mado about money. I couldn't tell her that I couldn't afford the apartment in Passy. It was her husband, quite by chance, who put me on to Ulrich.'

'Did you borrow a lot?'

'Less than seven thousand. But that's a lot when you're only on a thousand a month. One evening, when my wife was away visiting her sister in the Vendôme, Ulrich came to see me. He started threatening me. If I didn't pay at least the interest he would tell my employers, just for starters, then he'd send round the bailiffs. Can you see what a disaster that would have been? My bosses and my wife finding out at the same time?'

His tone was still calm and ironic.

'I was an idiot. I only wanted to smash his face in to teach him a lesson. But once he'd got a bloodied nose, he started screaming. I grabbed him round the neck. I felt strangely calm. It's not true that you lose your head at times like this. Quite the contrary. I don't think I've ever been as lucid in my life. I went to hire a car. I propped up the body to make it look as if I was carrying a friend who'd drunk too much. You know the rest.'

He almost reached out a hand to pick up a non-existent drink.

'So there it is. After that, you see life differently. Mado and I dragged on for another month or so. My wife got into the habit of having a go at me for my drinking. I had to give money to those two crooks. I told Basso everything. They say it's good to talk. That's just more fiction. The only thing that could help would be to start your life again from the beginning, right from the cradle.'

It was a droll remark, drolly expressed, and Maigret couldn't help smiling. He noticed Basso was smiling too.

'Stupid, I know, but it would have been even more stupid to have gone to the police and confessed that I'd killed a man.'

'So you made a little bolt-hole for yourself,' said Maigret.

'You have to survive somehow.'

It was a dismal story rather than a tragic one, perhaps

because of James's strange personality. It was a point of honour for him not to lose his cool. He shied away from the slightest hint of emotion.

So much so that he was the calmest person in the room, and seemed puzzled by the long faces of the other two.

'We men are such fools. Basso got himself into the same tangle – and with Mado again! Not even someone different! And of course it all went wrong. If I could have, I'd have confessed to killing Feinstein. Then we'd have been quits. But I wasn't even there. He behaved like an idiot right to the end. He ran away. I did what I could to help him.'

In spite of himself, there was a quaver in James's voice, so he stopped talking for a moment, until he was able to carry on in his familiar monotone:

'He should have told the truth from the start! Even now, he still wanted to hand over the 30,000 francs.'

'It would have been easier,' Basso grumbled. 'But now . . .'

'Now I'm free of it at last,' James interrupted him. 'Free of everything. This filthy mess of an existence, the office, the café, my . . .'

He was about to say 'my wife', his wife with whom he had not the slightest thing in common. His flat in Rue Championnet, where he sat reading any old thing just to pass the time. Morsang, where he would round up his companions for another drinking session.

He continued:

'I will be at peace.'

In prison! Somewhere he wouldn't be waiting for something that wasn't going to happen.

At peace in his little bolt-hole, eating, drinking and sleeping at the prescribed hour, breaking rocks on a chain gang or sewing up mailbags.

'What do you think, about twenty years?'

Basso was looking at him. He could hardly see him through the tears that welled up in his eyes and flowed down his cheeks.

'Stop it, James!' he cried out, his hands tensed into fists.

'Why?'

Maigret wiped his nose and tried mechanically to light his pipe, which was empty.

He felt he had never experienced such dark despair.

Not even dark. It was a dull, grey despair. A despair with no words of lament, no grimaces of pain.

A drinker's despair without the drunkenness – James never got drunk!

The inspector now understood what it was that brought them together every evening on the terrace of the Taverne Royale.

They would sit there together drinking, chatting aimlessly. And deep down James would hope that his companion would arrest him. He saw the suspicion emerging in Maigret and he nourished this suspicion, watched it grow. He waited.

'Another Pernod, old chap?'

He loved him like a friend who he hoped would one day deliver him from himself.

*

Maigret and Basso exchanged unreadable glances. James stubbed out his cigarette on the white table top.

'I just wish I could have done with it straight away. But there's the trial, all the questions, the tears, the sympathy.'

A police officer opened the door.

'The examining magistrate is here,' he announced.

Maigret hesitated, not quite knowing how to bring things to an end. He came forward and offered his hand with a sigh.

'Look, would you put in a good word for me? Just ask him if he can push it through quickly. I'll confess to everything. I just want to get in my bolt-hole as soon as possible.'

Then, as if to lighten the atmosphere, he added a parting remark:

'I'll tell you who'll be most upset. The waiter at the Taverne Royale. Will you go there and have one for me, inspector?'

Three hours later, Maigret was sitting on a train on his way to Alsace. Along the banks of the Marne he saw lots of bars just like the Two-Penny Bar, with their mechanical pianos in their wooden lean-tos.

He woke up early the next morning as the train pulled in. He saw a green-painted barrier in a little station bedecked with flowers.

Madame Maigret and her sister were anxiously scanning all the train doors.

And everything – the station, the countryside, his in-laws' house, the surrounding hills, even the sky – looked as fresh as if it had been scrubbed clean every morning.

'I bought you some varnished wood clogs yesterday in Colmar.'

Handsome yellow clogs that Maigret wanted to try on even before he had taken off his dark city clothes.

INSPECTOR MAIGRET

NIGHT AT THE CROSSROADS

GEORGES SIMENON

She stepped forwards, her silhouette slightly blurred in the dim light. She stepped forwards like a film star, or rather, like the perfect woman of an adolescent's dream.

And her brother stood by her as a slave stands near the sovereign he is sworn to protect.

On the outskirts of Paris, a sensational crime in an isolated neighbourhood becomes the focus of Maigret's investigation. But the strange behaviour of an enigmatic Danish aristocrat and his reclusive sister prove to be even more troubling.

Translated by Linda Coverdale

A CRIME IN HOLLAND

GEORGES SIMENON

'Just take a look,' Duclos said in an undertone, pointing to the scene all round them, the picture-book town, with everything in its place, like ornaments on the mantlepiece of a tidy housewife. Everyone here earns his living. Everyone's more or less content. And above all, everyone keeps his instincts under control, because that's the rule here, and a necessity if people want to live in society.'

Outsiders are viewed with suspicion in the small Dutch town of Delfzijl. Maigret, unable to speak the language and a stranger to their strict, church-going way of life, must unearth the sins at the heart of this seemingly respectable community.

Translated by Siân Reynolds

THE GRAND BANKS CAFÉ

GEORGES SIMENON

It was indeed a photo, a picture of a woman. But the face was completely hidden, scribbled all over in red ink. Someone had tried to obliterate the head, someone very angry. The pen had bitten into the paper. There were so many criss-crossed lines that not a single square millimetre had been left visible.

Captain Fallut's last voyage is shrouded in silence. To discover the truth about this doomed expedition, Maigret enters a remote, murky world of men on the margins of society; where fierce loyalties hide sordid affairs.

Translated by David Coward

INSPECTOR MAIGRET

OTHER TITLES IN THIS SERIES

www.penguin.com